797,885 Books
are available to read at

www.ForgottenBooks.com

Forgotten Books' App
Available for mobile, tablet & eReader

ISBN 978-1-331-83891-3
PIBN 10240455

This book is a reproduction of an important historical work. Forgotten Books uses state-of-the-art technology to digitally reconstruct the work, preserving the original format whilst repairing imperfections present in the aged copy. In rare cases, an imperfection in the original, such as a blemish or missing page, may be replicated in our edition. We do, however, repair the vast majority of imperfections successfully; any imperfections that remain are intentionally left to preserve the state of such historical works.

Forgotten Books is a registered trademark of FB &c Ltd.
Copyright © 2015 FB &c Ltd.
FB &c Ltd, Dalton House, 60 Windsor Avenue, London, SW19 2RR.
Company number 08720141. Registered in England and Wales.

For support please visit www.forgottenbooks.com

1 MONTH OF FREE READING

at

www.ForgottenBooks.com

By purchasing this book you are eligible for one month membership to ForgottenBooks.com, giving you unlimited access to our entire collection of over 700,000 titles via our web site and mobile apps.

To claim your free month visit:
www.forgottenbooks.com/free240455

* Offer is valid for 45 days from date of purchase. Terms and conditions apply.

Similar Books Are Available from
www.forgottenbooks.com

Emma: A Novel, Vol. 1 of 3
by Jane Austen

A Tale of Two Cities
by Charles Dickens

The Jungle Book
by Rudyard Kipling

Neæra
A Tale of Ancient Rome, by John W. Graham

A Selection from the World's Greatest Short Stories
Illustrative of the History of Short Story Writing, by Sherwin Cody

And Quiet Flows the Don, Vol. 1 of 4
A Novel, by Mikhail Aleksandrovich Sholokhov

Les Misérables (The Wretched)
A Novel, by Victor Hugo

Agatha Webb
by Anna Katharine Green

The Alhambra
Tales and Sketches of the Moors and Spaniards, by Washington Irving

All Shakespeare's Tales
by Charles Lamb

Anna Karénina
by Leo Tolstoy

At the Foot of Sinai
by Georges Clemenceau

The Case of Mr. Lucraft, and Other Tales, Vol. 1
by Walter Besant

The Chartreuse of Parma
by Stendhal

Cheveley, Vol. 1 of 2
Or The Man of Honour, by Rosina Bulwer Lytton

Children of the Mist
by Eden Phillpotts

A Cornish Droll
A Novel, by Eden Phillpotts

Dark Hollow
by Anna Katharine Green

The Deaf Shoemaker
by Philip Barrett

Doctor Hathern's Daughters
A Story of Virginia, in Four Parts, by Mrs. Mary Jane Holmes

ZENOBIA,

QUEEN OF PALMYRA.

VOLUME II.

ZENOBIA

QUEEN OF PALMYRA;

A Narrative,

FOUNDED ON HISTORY.

IN TWO VOLUMES.

BY THE
AUTHOR OF PATRIARCHAL TIMES.

VOL. II.

LONDON:
Printed by J. Dennett, Leather Lane, Holborn;
FOR F. C. AND J. RIVINGTON, ST. PAUL'S CHURCH YARD.

1814.

CONTENTS.

BOOK VII.

Elkanah in his study—The return of Antiochus from Rome—Zenobia informed of the sarcasms of Gallienus—Declares war against him—Zenobia's conquests—Her address to the people of Palmyra—Makes known to them the election of Aurelian to the Roman purple—Her interview with Longinus—Elkanah demands and obtains the government of Judea—A traveller arrives at Palmyra—The sepulchre of Odenathus 1

BOOK VIII.

Zenobia rejoins her family — Writes to Sapor—Holds a council, at which Paulus is made Procurator of Antioch—Theodosius attempts the conversion of the queen—An answer is received from Persia, with an account of the death of Valerian—Zenobia's emotion—The Patriarch takes advantage of this mournful intelligence to check her encreasing ambition—Urges baptism—His conversation with Septimia—Proposes a journey to Jerusalem 45

BOOK IX.

Preparations for the royal journey to Judea Omar the Arab takes charge of the young princes — Balbec — Damascus — Mount Lebanon—Sidon—Tyre—The lake of Tiberias—Capernaum—Zenobia's sorrowful reflections—She is encouraged by Theodosius—Nazareth—Mount Tabor—The hills of Gilboa—Jezreel—Cesarea—Samaria—Shiloh—Joppa—Idumea—The Red Sea—Bethlehem—Jerusalem—Mount Calvary—Theodosius blesses Zenobia and his Christian flock assembled on the Mount of Olives.......... 81

BOOK X.

Zenobia's return to Palmyra—Takes a survey of the suburbs of the city—Her reflections in the valley of the sepulchres—Is met by her father — The views of Elkanah considered — Through his means, Porphyry has accompanied him to Palmyra—Paulus returns from Antioch, and Theodosius is for a time removed —Heathenism revives—Antiochus urges the queen to new conquests—His advice is supported by many, and opposed by Orodes—The Roman province of Bithynia taken by Zabdas—Theodosius returns to Palmyra—The festive hall—The interview of the patriarch with Septimia and the young princes——The death of Septimia................ 149

BOOK XI.

Longinus reading to the queen his life of Odenathus, and eulogiums on Septimia—Theodosius appears—Reproves and threatens Zenobia—His remonstrances at length produce penitence—She promises the next day to acknowledge her abjuration of Judaism—Breaks her engagement made with the patriarch, in consequence of which he proposes for the Christians to leave Palmyra—The queen refuses her sanction—A meeting of the senate, at which Theodosius warns the Palmyrenians of the consequences of taking Bithynia—Morning—Public rejoicings in honour of Zenobia's new acquisitions—Olympic games The conquering generals enter Palmyra in triumph—Evening—The royal banquet, at which Zenobia is proclaimed by her subjects Empress of Rome, and her children assume the purple—Orodes incurs the displeasure of the queen, and leaves the hall—Claudian arrives from Rome—His intelligence produces universal dread and consternation 193

BOOK XII.

The battle of Imma, Zenobia defeated—Flies to Emessa—Palmyra puts itself in a state of defence—Orodes and others go and consult the oracle of Aphaca, return in despair—Zenobia and her vanquished forces regain Palmyra—Aurelian follows, and the siege begins—Theodosius offers to be the medium towards a restoration of peace—Zabdas returns, and at the gate of Palmyra wounds Aurelian—Zenobia receives a letter from Aurelian, requiring the surrender of the city—Her answer—Theodosius implores her not to send it; he is over-ruled and thrown into prison—The assault is renewed—Her succours being intercepted, Zenobia leaves Palmyra in the dead of night for Persia—Irenius requests of Elkanah the release of Theodosius—Account of the taking of Zenobia—Palmyra surrenders to Aurelian—The death of Longinus, Zabdas, and Orodes—Aurelian departs for Europe with his royal captive—Zenobia dies...... 223

ZENOBIA,

QUEEN OF PALMYRA.

BOOK VII.

ARGUMENT.

Elkanah in his study—The return of Antiochus from Rome—Zenobia informed of the sarcasms of Gallienus—Declares war against him—Zenobia's conquests—Her address to the people of Palmyra—Makes known to them the election of Aurelian to the Roman purple—Her interview with Longinus—Elkanah demands and obtains the government of Judea—A traveller arrives at Palmyra—The sepulchre of Odenathus.

THE doctrines of Zoroaster are more favourable to those of our nation, thought Elkanah, than is the persecuting spirit of polytheism: in Persia, the Hebrew finds rests and consideration—in Rome and Greece, none. Times have undergone great change, and my views must change accordingly. Had the bow-string been put on the neck of Meonius at the hour I advised, the world had been at peace; but now, as it appears to me that Persia in future would be a better ally than Rome, the world shall be at war. Rome refused to suffer my brethren to be redeemed from the mines of Egypt—— Egypt shall be ours. And he spread before him, on the table, various books and plans, over which he silently pondered until interrupted by the arrival of Caleb from Italy, whither he had attended Antiochus, who had been sent to inform the Roman senate of the late disastrous events in Syria.

Though anxious to learn the result of the embassy, Elkanah still adhered to his insolent practice of never questioning an inferior, and continued, scarcely noticing the entrance of Caleb, to turn over the leaves of a book of fortification. Caleb however, wilfully or naturally blind to the pride of the great Elkanah, kept him not long in suspense, but amply detailed every particular of their reception from Gallienus, the emperor. He had scarcely concluded, when Antiochus entered. Elkanah arose, and slowly traversed the room, the fever of indignation burning in his heart.—The words, said Caleb, were more than once repeated by Gallienus, and in the presence of his court; nay, he laughed the low ignoble laugh of buffoonery. 'Odenathus dead!' exclaimed he, ' and Herodian also! Husband, son, and nephew, in one day cut off! Three infant sovereigns, I grant, are more accommodating to the future views of that warlike, ambitious woman. I should have acted as she hath, wherefore, instead of resenting the deaths of my co-partners in the empire, I commend her policy.'

Base and abhorred insinuation! exclaimed Antiochus; words that could only issue from the lips of a Gallienus and his flatterers: but since we cannot punish, better they be buried in silence;

for what would be the feelings of my daughter, were she told of them. No, let her be only informed, what is strictly true, that the Roman empire mourns her loss; repeat not the words of its insulting master, lest from that hour, Zenobia vow eternal hatred to Rome, and thereby break that alliance on which our safety as a nation depends.

Thus had Antiochus unintentionally sealed the very measure against which he pleaded; the idea came upon the brain of Elkanah, and he hastened to put it in execution. As he left his palace to repair to that of the queen, Assisted by Persia, Parthia, India, and Arabia, said he, we may yet bridle the lips of Gallienus—and Judea no longer a Roman province! I shall yet govern Judea.

Entering the palace, he repaired to the private study of Zenobia, and found her engaged in writing, which employment alone convinced him that he stood not before a beauteous marble statue arrayed by the hands of fancy in robes of black;

that settled grief, that look of fixed despair, that hopeless indifference to all earthly enjoyments, time had rather encreased than diminished. She received her uncle courteously, and laying aside the pen, took up the needle.

Where is my sister? enquired Elkanah.—With the children in my cabinet.—Can we be overheard?—I know not.—Art thou at leisure to listen to me?—She bowed in silence.—Thy father Antiochus is returned from Rome—Rome condoles with thee and Palmyra; the people of Greece are also ready to mourn with the afflicted: one man alone mourned not; he was not afflicted—he was rejoiced.—Zenobia looked up.—Gallienus, the emperor, was seen to laugh; he more than laughed — he revelled. Caleb hath thus informed me: he powdered his hair with golden dust, fastened on his head a crown of brilliant rays, and called himself Apollo. In consequence of the pleasing news from Syria, he fought that day among the gladiators, attacked a castle built of melons, and slept on a bed of flowers.

Zenobia, scarcely conscious of Elkanab's discourse or presence, continued her work.—Doth not this account move thy anger?—No, my uncle: hadst thou told me, that on such an occasion, a Trajan had laughed—a Titus, a Vespasian had revelled, I had grieved: but a Gallienus! did he not even thus on hearing his father was a prisoner? Hath he ever made one attempt to redeem him? Were not some citizens of Rome put to death for seeking the emperor's father among the ransomed captives from Persia? Thy account resembles that of him, who, after the murder of Seneca, told another that Nero had stabbed his favourite elephant.

I have only related to thee the *actions* of Gallienus, replied Elkanah; wilt thou hear his *words?* He was heard in full senate to boast that it was his hand that made thy husband king; that he alone may give crowns, and take crowns away; and he is at this moment considering on whom he shall bestow the crown of Palmyra.—Elkanah had gained his point; that pure and rosy blood which had not for many months appeared either in the cheeks or lips of Zenobia, now rushed wildly into them — types of innocence and beauty securing the thrones given them by nature and Odenathus. But when Elkanah seizing his advantage, recounted to her, word for word, the remarks of Gallienus, his insinuations, his sarcasms, his open accusation of her having been accessary to the murder of her husband and his son, the colour again forsook her countenance, her eyes were cast upwards, and her joined hands raised as if in speechless agony invoking the spirits of Odenathus and Herodian to come down in her justification.

Thou Father of heaven, who witnessed what then passed in her heart, canst alone tell what that heart for a few moments suffered! could words express her wounded feelings! These were ever best expressed by silence—but the result of that silence!

Thus is our globe, thus mankind agitated and ruled by the private passions of a few solitary individuals. Gallienus at Rome but made one perhaps thoughtless observation, accompanied by the low grimace of a jester; this being brought from Rome to Palmyra, was exaggerated to Zenobia; and the same day the roads from Palmyra to every quarter of the world, were covered with couriers and messengers.

To Egypt a declaration was sent, and Zabdas, with seventy thousand men, (militia, Syrians, and northern troops) were the bearers; it set forth that Zenobia, the descendant of Cleopatra, who last swayed that sceptre, wrested from her by Roman tyranny, now claimed her right, and that Zabdas would sustain her title to that throne. Elkanah, with gifts of peace and an honourable escort, was dispatched to Ecbatana, with proposals of amity to Sapor, the successor of Cyrus, the son of Artaxerxes, king of kings, and rightful possessor of the triple diadem. Victorinus and Balista were empowered to raise sixty thousand Armenians and Arabians; and Antiochus was sent to Asia Minor, there to make known the pretensions of Zenobia.

Egypt was conquered, and Zabdas returned to Palmyra, accompanied by the great Timagenes of Ptolemais, who, having declared for the interests of Syria, came to receive his reward, one look of the Syrian queen. Elkanah came back from Persia with Statirus, bringing gifts of peace and friendship. Victorinus encamped his new levies beyond the hills of Thapsacus, and Zenobia, at the head of her armies, went to meet Heraclian, the Roman general, who was on his way to attack Parthia; not now the wife, the nurse, the guardian, the shield of Odenathus, but the spirit of Odenathus itself. Zenobia fought, and Heraclian fled; and to his flight was owing the death of Gallienus. To avoid the fate of unsuccessful commanders, Heraclian hid his dishonoured head in Scythia, where conspiring with the disaffected, a Roman named Claudius was proclaimed emperor, and Gallienus was assassinated beneath the walls of Milan.

Claudius, unlike his predecessor, a man of virtue, valour, wisely politic, and honourably prudent, at his election commanded the sword to be sheathed. In vain was he urged to check the alarming progress of the Syrian arms—in vain, at his assumption of the purple, the senate five times cried out, Oh, Emperor Claudius, deliver us from the Palmyrenians! and again seven times, Oh, Claudius, rescue us from Zenobia and Victoria! he answered not a word, gave no promise, no explanation of his conduct. Leaving Tetricus to rule the west, and Zenobia the east, he turned his arms against the Goths and Scythians; and thus in two years did Zenobia, without opposition, render herself mistress of

Egypt, Abyssinia, Ethiopia, Media, Parthia, and Mesopotamia.

Oh, hasten onward, hasten to the accomplishment of all things—pass with the rapidity of the conquerors themselves, over events like these; war is war, and subjugations are all alike—dwell not on such · but, arriving at an interval of peace, there pause, there stop to breathe, and look around; stop with delight on the fruits of peace, and linger with pleasure when describing the progress of science, industry, arts, and knowledge. Say, how great, how extensive is now the kingdom of Palmyrene, stretching from Euphrates to the Propontis, and from Mount Taurus to the southern limits of Ethiopia! How flourishing now Palmyra, the emporium of the East, who with one hand collects in the Indies its gold and pearls, its ivory, silks, and spices, and with the other scatters them over the West, thereby encreasing her own wealth to a boundless extent! The Palmyra of this day no more resembles the Palmyra which, some years back, Zenobia wept over, than the Rome of Romulus could be compared to the Rome of Augustus Cæsar. A chain of towns extending from it through the empire (itself the glorious centre), gradually expanding circle after circle, until now far, oh, far beyond its natural mountain-barriers, it hath attained the summit of earthly magnificence!

Form in thy imagination two men crossing a boundless desert, hastening to overtake their caravan gone on before, watched by a plundering horde of Arabs. The first appears in sight, clad in a simple shepherd coat: his person dignified, firm, and manly; every polished limb, every feature displaying health, grace, and good-will; he looks at the Arab, and smiling, points to his coat, his scrip, and shepherd staff, and passes unmolested. The second stranger approaches, a superb colossal figure, moving heavily, encumbered with his own weight, his richly embroidered garments, his gold, and precious stones: he looks around with eye askance, all cautious suspicion and fears; he trembles at the neighing of the wild ass—he starts at the leaf blown to his feet by the wind; he sees the springing Arab; his feet are entangled in the fringe of his raiment—he strives to escape, and falls. Such, oh, Palmyra! wert thou under Odenathus—such art thou now.

In full assembly of the people on her return from the conquest of Asia Minor, of which Bithynia alone now remained to Rome, Zenobia addressed her female subjects expressly summoned on the occasion—Let no woman henceforth presume to follow my example, or imitate as heretofore a conduct which circumstances now compel me to pursue, unless placed in the station I am placed in. As a daughter, my parents here present are my witnesses; as a wife, you all witnessed; as a mother—never shall my hand resign this sword of Odenathus, until these boys have strength to use it, and then will I gladly stand beneath its shadow; by me shall this shield of defence be held before them, until nature and the blood that fills their veins bids them no longer hide behind it. This throne was not the gift of the Roman, but yours, O Palmyrenians; you gave it to Odenathus, and never will you see these children of Odenathus torn from it! The sword fell from her trembling grasp, the shield was eagerly caught from her by Timagenes, the Egyptian, for he had seen a tear fall upon that shield, and while Herennianus and Timolaus, her eldest boys, clasped her knees, she folded Vaballathus, the youngest, to her breast.

Again recovering herself, she looked around upon the multitude with the pure affection of a mother. Do not misconstrue my words, she said, or be offended, but of a truth, there are three species of beings on earth, men, women, and sovereigns—you are all relatively connected, can understand each other, but who can judge my feelings? Every one present, nor sex nor age considered, appear to me a son, a daughter, all the orphaned children of Odenathus; then to your protection I give the rights and persons of these your orphaned brothers. The peace and prosperity we have long enjoyed is perhaps on the eve of expiring, for Claudius, whose procrastinated attack I well understood, and for which I was ever prepared, is dead.—Dead! exclaimed many, whilst others, informed of the news, remained silent—And the Roman army, she continued, hath elected a new emperor. I will describe, do you name him. Born of the lowest parentage, his manners those of the roughest soldier—proud, false, determined, cruel; from the ranks made a centurion, tribune, prefect of a legion, inspector of the camp, general of the frontiers, commander of cavalry, consul, emperor.—She ceased, and a thousand voices exclaimed, Aurelian!

Arm then, ye Palmyrenians! added Zenobia; sleep with sword in hand, and buckler on arm! hang the breast-plate at the corner of the bed, and place upon your pillow the martial trumpet! Let Aurelian be the first to throw the dart of defiance, and be you ready to charge. If the Roman eagle attack the Syrian palm, heaven will fight in the cause of innocence, and Aurelian learn that the eastern empire yields not to the western.

Another year elapsed, and all was profound tranquillity. Aurelian, intent on overpowering the northern barbarians; in destroying all pretenders to the purple, in rebuilding the walls of Rome, and settling its civil government, appeared to have forgotten that there was a Palmyra in the world, a Zenobia in existence; he was never heard to speak of either, and thus the future flame of destruction was as yet hidden in the flint.

Zenobia now in her own person, queen, emperor, general, and judge, governed with admirable wisdom: she decided on all things after mature consultation with age and experience, but from her decision there was no appeal. Thus, wonderfully in her own eyes, permitted to retain her conquests (for she could not be mistaken in the character of Aurelian), she devoted herself to the further embellishment of her empire, the happiness of her subjects, and the education of her sons· their religious instruction was undertaken by Septimia and herself, occasionally assisted by Elkanah and Paulus, the judaising Bishop of Antioch; Longinus was appointed governor of the elder prince, and Porphyry of Tyre that of the younger; and until the arrival of these, the one from Greece, and the other from Italy, Antiochus himself undertook the direction of their studies.

Zenobia, for the use of her sons, drew up an epitome of eastern history, and at their request, began a translation of a Greek author into the Syrian language; thus dividing her time between public and private business, both equally interesting to her heart. Religious duties, affairs of state, exercise on horseback or a chariot, reviews, literature, and amusements, were her daily occupations from sun-rise until midnight; and faithfully she adopted Odenathus' custom of taking an accurate survey every spring of part of the empire. In these her sons latterly accompanied her, and thus the remotest subject of each realm had the opportunity of becoming personally known to their youthful kings, who were taught to look forward even beyond those remote limits to future conquests. My arm, said Zenobia, hath accomplished enough; I leave the rest to yours.

On their return from Asia Minor, of which they had visited every newly gained province, Zenobia found Longinus arrived from Greece, and Claudian from Rome, attracted thence by his love for the beauteous widow of Herodian.

Elkanah was the first who discovered to the queen that Herodian was forgotten of Victoria. Passing through the royal anti-chamber, he beheld Victoria, and she was not alone; Claudian was near her: Elkanah glanced at both as he passed—'Tis well, he said; all proceeds as I would have it: my agent at Rome hath been faithful—that blush was the blush of love:—a second marriage removes her from the throne, and my niece Zenobia remains sole sovereign.

And where is Porphyry? asked the queen of Longinus, thy former disciple, him by thee so much extolled? Why did he not accompany thee?—He was not worthy, replied Longinus, for by abstinence and other philosophical indulgences, he hath become but the walking shadow of wisdom; nay, I mistook him for the ghost of Plato himself, and feared his appearance at this court should terrify Timolaus into ignorance and hatred of philosophy.—If his health hath suffered from study and confinement, replied Zenobia, the soft air of Palmyra at his age might be of service. Write to him, and express my wishes.—He will not heed them, queen, answered Longinus; for in my presence, he interlined my first letter with an essay on rhetoric and grammar, and when I repeated thy royal invitation, he began to criticize the critic.

Thou art envious of his fame, fearful that the genius of the scholar will eclipse that of the master; but as thou hast failed in persuading Porphyry to accept the charge of Timolaus, thou shalt be burdened with both the princes; and as I suffer no idlers at this court, lest thy time should not be amply filled up, thou art from this hour my privy counsellor and secretary.—Secretary, dear queen, most willingly, but I will not be responsible for the results of thy council.—And on what hast thou been employed whilst in Greece? for it is easier for Zabdas to sleep without a sword in his hand, as thou remain awake without a pen in thine What is the subject of thy late writings?—Eulogium, replied Longinus, his voice saddening to a sigh; on his lip trembled the name of Odenathus— he could not pronounce it, nor was it requisite, for where soul comprehends soul, words are unnecessary. The eyes of Zenobia were filled with tears as she hastily rose to leave him; he fell at her feet, and continued to kiss her robe, until she gave him her hand. If, she said—and her voice was choked and trembling— if thou dost wish more information of latter events—such as a bosom friend, a wife, a fond one, can alone give—the many little private anecdotes overlooked by the world, which yet stamp the character, apply to me; I best can furnish thee—I that——Wholly overcome, she burst into tears, and breaking from him, rushed to her cabinet, where, unconscious that any one was present, she threw herself on a couch, and sobbed and wept with renewed grief.

A gentle footstep approached her, she felt the soft pressure of the hand, and without taking the veil, drenched in tears, from her eyes, said, My mother, it is nothing; but this is the first time Longinus and I have met since I lost him.—Here is thy uncle, my child, replied Septimia, who hath long been waiting to see and speak with thee.

Zenobia looked up, and rising cold and severe, turned to where sat Elkanah. This room of all my empire I alone reserve sacred to my mother and myself; even my father hath never crossed yon threshold, and were my sons to appear at it contrary to command, they would be long debarred my presence.—Elkanah in silence rose, and would have quitted the place, had not Septimia prevented him. Am I permitted to make known the cause of my trespass? Zenobia was silent, and he continued, Judea is thine. She looked astonished Not by force of arms, but voluntary friendship; the children of our nation, rescued from Egypt by Zabdas, have settled in Samaria, and at their instigation, the whole country from Cesaræa Philippi to the antient Beersheba, has secretly declared for thy interests, and placed itself under thy protection.

This intelligence, replied the pleased Zenobia, is most gratifying, for unless I could have obtained bloodless possession, I never had acquired it, being resolved not to carry the sword into the land of my forefathers. Thou, said Elkanah, thou, greater than Cyrus or Artaxerxes, now perform thy promise. Have I the government of Judea?—She hesitated, on which he exclaimed, in anger, Dost thou retract? Make me a Zerubbabel, an Ezra, a Nehemiah, or I quit thy council and thy presence ever. He placed his hand on the door, and waited her reply. Septimia caught his gown, and cast a supplicating look at Zenobia, who, thus appealed to, replied, smiling, I may invest thee with the commission with which they were invested, but to make thee a Zerubbabel, an Ezra, or a Nehemiah, is beyond my power.

Had an inferior uttered this taunt,

the form of Elkanah would have swelled to great magnitude, but coming from the lips of a queen, although his niece, his attention at that moment was engaged in unfastening and tightening his girdle.— In all that these men did, continued Zenobia, they consulted the honour of God —whose dost thou consult?—And was it for this was planned the oracle of Apollo? demanded Elkanah; for this that thou wert nurtured in Judaism, and wedded to one whose heart thou didst at pleasure mould? All this performed by me, and what is my reward?—The pleasure of triumphing over the oracle of Balbec, answered Zenobia—the gratified ambition of seeing thy kinswoman raised to empire: ambition and emulation thus satisfied, yet seek greater reward?

Recal the Jews, rebuild Jerusalem, exclude the present city, and restore the ancient foundations. — Will they obey the call? enquired Zenobia. Can Jerusalem be restored? Since the reign of Adrian, when the ploughshare went over the earth, and tore up those foundations, what hath been its state?—Canst thou not inform me?—Then be informed. The new city Elia, built by Adrian, though not in the same situation, hath at this hour a Roman garrison: one quarter, that of Calvary, is inhabited chiefly by Christians, and governed by a patriarch, a man of piety and zeal, of whom all here have heard, named Theodosius; unlike our Paulus of Antioch, that proud and superb prelate, Theodosius is a Christian, according to his own definition of the word—humble and forbearing where worldly concerns are the object—fervid and impassioned when preaching his doctrine. If that neither this patriarch nor his brethren must by my order be disturbed, how can thy intentions be executed?

This then, exclaimed Elkanah, no longer able to controul the vindictive passions of his nature, ever roused by the name of Christian—this is the real

motive that my suit is rejected. Odenathus shewed but too much partiality for
that sect, but thou art become yet more
partial. Thy cherishing kindness to the
Christians of this city hath been undissembled, thy indulgence to their preju-
dices noticed; instead of the scourge and
the stone, many and great largesses from
the treasury have been made to build
and repair their churches, although they
ever refuse to contribute to that treasury,
and daily murmur at paying tribute.—
Would, said Zenobia, that my Jewish
subjects paid it as readily. I have been
among these Christians, and have ever
remarked peace, order, loyalty, and good
fellowship; they appear not possessing,
but hoping, enduring, and unless they
rebel against public authority, shall meet
with no molestation from me.—Both
Jews and Pagans are daily by their persuasion perverted to Christianity, remarked Elkanah.—Be it so; I infringe
not on the jurisdiction of heaven, replied

Zenobia: provided they are good citizens and faithful subjects, they are entitled to my protection.

Elkanah took a blank parchment from the sleeve of his robe, and spread it before her. Here sign thy name, he said, and fix thy seal: armed with this thy commission, I collect forces, and raise supplies; when known to be thy will, the empire flocks to my government, and as in the days of Herod, pours forth its treasures to rebuild the temple. Judea ere long shall glory in her new Jerusalem. I fear, said Zenobia, she will not long glory in her new governor. Elkanah let fall the roll, whilst Septimia displeased that thus a man of his age, her brother, and Zenobia's uncle should endure the rebuke of youth, without having the liberty to resent it, made signs to Elkanah to sit down, and quitting Zenobia, she went over and placed herself at his side: and O, how quickly faded the authority of sovereign before that of mother!

I do not, said Septimia, as thou, Zenobia, art well aware, understand these things, but this, my brother hath often made me observe — Thou hast built several splendid cities throughout the land, some called after thy name, yet it appears, art perversely disinclined to raise one stone of that holy city of our forefathers,—thou hast collected together Syrian fugitives from various quarters of the world, yet hast not made one attempt to assemble the remnant of our nation, to make it a strong people, that the Lord may reign in Sion ever. The Hebrew is now scattered as dew among the Gentiles waiting to be gathered, and thou, oh queen! dost refuse to be the gatherer, thy uncle is scoffed at, and I ⸺

Zenobia, starting from her seat, rushed to the knee of Septimia—My mother! if thou dost proceed thus agitated—retain, if thou wilt, words of kindness, but utter not one of displeasure, for that can never be recalled.—From the hour I first could distinguish thee from the world, never did I witness thee thus—thou callest me queen; yet which is greater, the being that wears the crown, or that, at whose feet it is laid?—And, as she spoke, she took the diadem from her brow, and placing it at the feet of Septimia, hid her face upon her knee.—When again she raised her head, Elkanah was gone; the roll lay on the floor: she took it up and hastily signing it, and affixing her seal, placed it in the hands of her mother, who, after a silent embrace, departed in search of Elkanah.

Seated beside a spring without the walls of Palmyra, behold an aged stranger and a traveller, or rather pilgrim, for his worldly possessions are little more than what thou seest; *his scrip, his staff, his long loose garment, and his sandals:* yet, though aged, meet but his eye, and therein thou wilt see the fire of youth blended with the simplicity of childhood—weary, trembling, and dejected, his sighs are frequent, and his movements slow—to allay the painful burning of his feet he puts off his sandals and bathes them in the rapid stream; then opens his scrip and takes from it scanty remains of bread, which he steeps in the brook at its source.

Thou givest food to the ravens, thou wilt not let me perish; thou cloathest the grass of the field, which to-day is, and to-morrow is cut down; thou wilt not lead me into the snare.—Oh, thou who kindledst the spark within me, who fanned it to bright enthusiasm, who made me quit beloved Jerusalem, and guarding me from the extremity of peril, hath brought me to this unknown Palmyra—Oh, convince me, ere I enter on my mission, that this deep depression of spirit proceeds alone from natural infirmity—Yet should our little band of brethren dwelling here have been cut off, and no brother here to receive me! Should persecution have risen within these heathen walls—what am I? What am I! he repeated, a candidate for the crown of martyrdom.—Here do I rest, here my labours commence, here end my toilsome steps, here at Palmyra begins my most important task. Oh thou, who touched the lips of prophets, give persuasion to mine; inspire me with thy grace, and strengthen me to perform thy sacred will.

'Whilst yet seated, two soldiers passed, unheeded at first by the stranger, but he escaped not their notice; he was hastily questioned as to his name and occupation; when, without waiting a reply, they cautioned him to remove from that spot, and passed rapidly on their way. He fastened on his sandals, and taking up his scrip and staff arose, but ere he could reach the nearest gate of the city, he beheld an approaching army—swift as the shadow of a cloud gliding over the earth, the troops in awful silence spread over the extensive field; no shout arose; not a murmur was heard; no command given; they stood as if a host of spirits, or men changed to stone by the hand of enchantment.

How wonderful to the traveller, that every eye should rest on one spot! with intense eagerness the faces of the whole army appeared turned to a small postern, near where one of the rivers entered the city beneath a grated archway: where for a time all were held in still suspense, the least motion was discernible, and he perceived two men of superior dress and stature, pass with silent dignity through the yet immoveable ranks: in their rounds they approached so near the spot where he stood, that he could discern their features, and he read therein anxiety and deep concern; these were soon joined by a third coming from the postern, whom they hastened to meet: in consequence of his tidings a general murmur arose, and the traveller caught these words—The queen comes not; another dawn is past, and the review is again deferred until to-morrow.

The ranks were broken, tents pitched,

and fires kindled throughout the field; the stranger tarried no longer; he hastened to the gate of the city, but, on being challenged by the centinel, was refused admittance — he knew not the watch-word, he told not whence he came — when asked his name, he hesitated; and when desired to say of what country, was silent.—Thus he stood, when Zabdas, having left orders with his officers, quitted the field and came towards the gate: he was passing, carelessly speaking to the centinel as he entered, when his arm was caught by the traveller, who, in the accent of supplication, said, I pray thee, suffer me to follow thee —The general turned and looked upon him; I did possess passports, but in my way hither was robbed in the desert.—If thou wilt not suffer me to enter, being wholly exhausted, here I perish.—We do not thus admit strangers into a fortified city, replied Zabdas, but inform me who, and what thou art, and I will take the responsibility of admitting thee on myself.—

The traveller drew near to Zabdas, and, unheard by the centinels, whispered four simple words.—Oh, how irresistible is he, who is conducted by the hand of God!—Zabdas with respect, nay veneration, stepped back, and looking at his countenance, remained not an instant more in doubt—with all the generous courtesy of the accomplished soldier, he raised his hand to his helmet in graceful salutation, and led the stranger forward:—they entered, and the gates were closed.

The hour of public audience is returned, when the throne being filled, petitions are received or laid aside for future examination—some are instantly granted, others as instantly rejected—when justice is administered, maidens are portioned, youth rewarded, the injured redressed, and age is made honourable. The council-room is full, the seats of the judges thronged, the area crowded, but the throne is empty: on that empty throne every distant eye is fixed, whilst the nearer sight watches a folding door to the left.—In expectation of the opening of that door, the culprit trembles, old age sickens of hope deferred; the impatient child tires its widowed mother with enquiries of, Which is the queen?—the vexed and ardent youth, closer grasps the withdrawing hand of his betrothed, saying, Yet one moment longer and she will come;—in vain the gently-resisting virgin, shrinking, answers, But yet she doth not come.

The traveller, standing near the entrance, looks wondering upon this assemblage of infancy, childhood, youth, prime, and age; this mingled concourse of beauty, grace, valour, wisdom, and learning—all are motionless—for the beautiful, the chaste, the wise, the learned, the valiant is not here.—Antiochus, ascending a few steps of the throne, spake aloud: here on this humble foot-stool of royalty, have you often suffered me to become the proxy of your sovereign, let me now preside and strive to exercise the power of her, whose presence this day you look for in vain.

They listened, and in a few minutes, himself and the stranger were the only persons in the hall.

The evening is come when Claudian, the gallant Roman, shall wed the lovely Victoria, Herodian's widow; the interior of the palace blazes with artificial light of various hues, and fancifully disposed; the marble walls and pillars are hung with cloth of gold, and garlands of flowers; the galleries are thronged with all that Palmyra can boast of beauty and valour, for Claudian is most brave, and Victoria (Zenobia being away) the loveliest present.—The traveller is here also, and he perceives that attention is not engrossed by the magnificence of surrounding objects: not on the band of blooming children which strew the ground with flowers, nor on the female procession who with tabret, song, and dance, approach the centre of the hall—no; attention, universal attention is directed to one spot, one dark narrow passage near the minstrels' gallery—the hand of the musician hangs over his lyre, ready to strike the chord—the virgin band but wait the signal to pour forth the strains of melody, whilst Claudian pants with anxious bliss for the moment, when a voice shall say, Victoria may be thine.

A fluttering is observed at the entrance of the passage, expectation rises, and a murmur of—The queen! when disappointment fell on all—a female slave alone appeared, who beckoned Claudian, she spoke and vanished.

With undissembled anger he turned to the multitude, and waving his hand for them to disperse and retire to their own homes, said, in the sullen voice of discontent—The marriage is deferred until to-morrow.

How sad, how solemn, all within these high sepulchral walls of black unpolished stone!—Chamber of death! from the ceiling hangs the never-dying funeral lamp: in the centre lie the embalmed remains of Odenathus (alone admitted to the honour of sepulture within the walls of the city), and near the white tomb, stands on a low pedestal, the statue of that murdered prince.—Behold, in the whitest marble, how admirably represented his limbs, his features, grace, and majesty!—Doth it not seem the embodied spirit, mourning over its late human habitation?

Here also behold Zenobia, his tomb her couch, the base of his statue her table: hooks her only companion. For these, have the senate, the throne, and the field been three weeks neglected: for hither each morn, on leaving her bed, hath she thus long repaired and immured herself; nor father, mother, children, or subject daring to intrude upon her solitude.

How my soul dreads, yet longs for that hour, when doubt shall be ended! when this bewildered veil before my eyes shall be snatched away, and I behold the path I ought to pursue: when my now wavering belief shall be fixed incapable of change.—How dreadful to my enlightened mind hath ever appeared the worship of the Pagan, and may there not be a like difference between the faith I now profess, and that to which I am called?—Soul of Odenathus tell me! leave the bosom of heaven, and come and teach me truth! Would that this apostle were arrived, for reading often bewilders judgment, unsettling one belief without confirming another; and when he doth arrive, nor Paulus nor Elkanah shall step between him and me, ere doubt be for ever banished.—Let him open all his soul, explain his doctrine, solve every mystery, remove every objection, make clear his gospel, and the consequence be on my own head, whether to accept or reject the terms of salvation he professes to hold out to me.

O, recal those words, recal those awful words! exclaimed a voice, nor thus hazard invoking a malediction on thy head.—Zenobia started, she turned and saw at the entrance of the sepulchre the aged stranger. — Be not alarmed, he said, it is not a spirit that addresses thee, as this wasted form might lead thee to imagine, but one expected.—Alarmed! replied Zenobia, I know not the word, but I am versed in anger, and am prone to punish; thou art not a Palmyrenian, or thou hadst not thus offended—Who art thou?

Again the traveller repeated the same four words, which had operated like a charm on Zabdas; those four words, which now disarmed Zenobia of all pride and resentment.— Theodosius, Patriarch of Jerusalem.

Thou wonderest, yet I am he; didst thou not expect me?—Three weeks back didst not receive letters and other important documents, apprizing thee of my coming?—Is it my present appearance only that creates surprise, and brings over thy countenance, that slight shade of disdain and incredulity?

Art thou the Theodosius, of whom I have heard speak: the apostle of the Christians; the patriarch of Calvary?— I am.—Yet thus; and to me!—To thee, Zenobia, thinkst thou then, O queen! that I tempted the Almighty to work miracles in my favour, and left Jerusalem thus?—No; I left it with servants, guides, horses, and treasures; but, on this side Lebanon, was by the Arabs plundered of all, and in the remainder of my journey the Almighty miraculously preserved me.

All awe and wonder, Zenobia gazed and listened: she watched him searching in the folds of his gown, and saw him take thence a small book, now his only treasure.—Here are my credentials, he said: compare this signature and seal with those already in thy possession, and look upon this book—the Gospel:—is it not the counterpart of that I sent thee?—Zenobia examined all, and pointing to the open page of the book she had been reading at his entrance, said, This for the last twenty days hath been my sole study: a Greek Testament, the Acts, the Epistles, and the Revelations. Here in this chamber of the dead, in solitude, in darkness, and in silence, have I at thy desire, read and compared, prayed and meditated.

It was not by my desire, replied Theodosius, that thou retiredest to' solitude and darkness; it was not my advice to immure thyself in the chamber of the dead, and thus to abandon thy family and people: I entered Palmyra at break of day, and it is now sun-set; in that short space of time I have heard thy armies murmur; have seen thy subjects mutinous, justice in thy hall of council unsatisfied, and worship neglected: such are not the lessons taught in those pages.—But thou didst advise retirement and meditation, interrupted Zenobia.—I advised both, replied the Patriarch, but it was the retirement of thy closet, there to read, to reflect, to compare, when the business of state, and the duties of a mother, permitted thee to absent thyself from the senate and thy children.

I now leave thee to visit my Christian brethren of this city, and thanks, O queen, and thou, O departed Odenathus, for thy kindness to them; we of Jerusalem heard all, or I had not been here.—This interview was not intentional, I walked this way, not knowing whither it led, conceal not, therefore, my coming, for no mystery must attend our meetings: I come, in the open face of day, to preach the Gospel to Palmyra, to preach it alike to Jew and Gentile.—To-morrow I enter on my mission, and to-morrow at our church be present all that will, thy mother, thy children, and court. Thy example, Zenobia, hath gained many Jewish proselytes; be thyself first converted, and a tenfold number may be added to the Christian faith.

END OF THE SEVENTH BOOK.

ZENOBIA,
QUEEN OF PALMYRA.

BOOK VIII.

ARGUMENT.

Zenobia rejoins her family—Writes to Sapor—Holds a Council, at which Paulus is made Procurator of Antioch—Theodosius attempts the conversion of the Queen—An answer is received from Persia, with an account of the death of Valerian—Zenobia's emotion—The Patriarch takes advantage of this mournful intelligence to check her encreasing ambition—Urges baptism—His conversation with Septimia—Proposes a journey to Jerusalem.

THUS doth the sower sow the seed: some falleth by the way-side, some upon stony ground, other on good ground—this fell among thorns; the word was heard, but soon, weighty cares of state, deceit, and misrepresentation choked it, and it became unfruitful.

Zenobia restored to her family and people, made ample amends for her late temporary absence. On Septimia were bestowed the tenderest caresses, such as the delightful solitudes of Zaantha witnessed; on her children such soft endearments that mothers only can bestow, because only valued when given by mothers: taking the youngest on her lap, she let the two elder hang upon her, and patiently smiling, listened to the wonderful events that had occurred since they had seen her.—I have come to the resolution, said the elder, when master of Rome, of killing all the gladiators, and thus putting an end to their horrid combats. —Herennianus, said Zenobia, is willing to cut up evil by the roots, and then pointed out a more humane method of executing his will.—And my little Timolaus? said she, fondly tracing in his, the features of Odenathus. Timolaus, replied Septimia, appears to aspire to no higher vocation than that of a vine-dresser, for all his hours, unengaged with his masters, he spends with me in the vineyard at New Zaantha: And there, said Timolaus, dear aged mother Septimia, is causing to be made for herself a new sepulchre in the rock, and we are all to be buried therein. Hath this, indeed been thy employment, my mother? asked Zenobia.—Could I put thy valued gift of Zaantha to a more sacred purpose? asked Septimia.—To die in thy arms and be buried at Zaantha, were ever the fondest wishes of my heart. There also will I sleep in death, said Zenobia.

Perceiving that the eyes of her mother were fixed upon her in tender examination, she enquired the cause.— Where now, asked Septimia, is thy features' fair and rosy hue, the freshness of which, when thou wert young, I took such delight to preserve? thy late absence makes the change to me most observable, for truly, Zenobia, one shade more of glowing brown, and thy complexion will, in darkness, resemble that of Odenathus.—Then, yet a few suns, Zenobia replied, and it shall wear that beloved shade.

And where is Longinus? Here at present, great queen, he replied, coming from the aperture of a window, where he was conversing with Antiochus, but an hour more and I had been on my return to Greece, since I find my post of secretary only a name.—Then instantly enter on thy duty, she answered, and recal my uncle, Elkanah, from Judea: that done, go to my cabinet, and among other papers, seek a letter addressed to Sapor the king; copy it, and have it dispatched at the third hour to Persia. t

The marriage of Victoria and Claudian was celebrated the same day, the next was appointed for giving audience, and the third for the review of the troops. Zenobia only left her couch to repair to the senate, the city, or the field, and only quitted them to sink upon her couch, oppressed with fatigue. The sacred writings, until then her sole companion, she knew not where were removed, and thus again plunged into worldly affairs, Theodosius was wholly forgotten. From their meeting in the sepulchre of Odenathus to this day, now many weeks, they have not met. The council, consisting of the heads of the Palmyrenian tribes have taken their seats; the heathen population is represented by sixty men, the Jewish by ten; and the Christian by one, and that one, on this day is Theodosius.'

All dignity and self-command, Zenobia answered and listened to the seventy, but when she came to that one, her eye sank beneath his penetrating look, and she strove in vain to conceal what passed within her; his calm, his mild, and silent reproach brought the blush of shame upon her cheek.

Attempting to recover the unabashed firmness of majesty, she at length observed, that the procurator of Antioch was dead, and that it being a post of singular honour and importance, lucrative in itself and possessing very extensive jurisdiction, she was tempted to give it to a Christian, in consideration, that the sect of the Nazarenes was first named Christian at Antioch; and whilst she spoke, she fixed her eyes on Theodosius. He read her thoughts.—Is it thy real design to bestow the dignity on me, he asked, or dost thou only hold out a false lure to seek the bent of my inclinations? This open demand, above all artifice, all design, made artifice deeper blush, and Zenobia thus called upon, answered with unusual timidity: It is thine, holy father. —No; replied Theodosius, I do not accept it, for my post is here; in Palmyra are centered all my desires, desires easily gratified, that consist in change of raiment, simple food, and a shelter from the weather: all these I have at the Christian college, and more I do not want.

The seventy and one looked upon the patriarch; he stood not long their gaze, for having obtained that which he was deputed to ask (a charter for building a new church at Edessa), he paid the customary tribute and retired. He was no sooner gone, than Paulus rising, addressed

Zenobia: I would be procurator at Antioch.—First inform me, replied the queen, what thou art at present, for on every council day, I have observed thee occupy a different side of the hall; the last but one thou wert seated on my left-hand, a Polytheist; the day ensuing, thou stoodst facing me, a Christian; and now upon my right-hand thou risest from among these, a Jew: thou art already bishop of Antioch, and ecclesiastical and secular power may not be blended in one person.

This sentence of rejection gave rise to a tedious and learned debate, which ended in the wish of Paulus being granted, and he departed to enter on possession. Thus was removed unconsciously, yet at his own prayer, the great enemy to Christianity; for who so dangerous to the cause of truth, as the heretical, the apostate Christian? and such was the luxurious Paulus of Sarmosata.—So works Providence, so is man's will left free and unbiassed!

Weary and mortified, Zenobia escaped from the council and repaired to her summer chamber; where seated at the marble fountain, at the upper end, she found her mother, to whom Herennianus was reading aloud: unwilling to interrupt them, she made a sign for the prince to proceed, and taking a book from an adjoining recess, was placing herself in a distant corner, when the door opened and a page announced the patriarch of Jerusalem.

Shame and mortification fled the countenance of Zenobia, and she stood waiting his approach, whilst Septimia all amazement at an honour never paid by the queen to any subject, watched with curiosity for the entrance of him who claimed it, and when Theodosius did enter, the prince lowered his book, and Septimia herself involuntarily arose.

I am pardoned, holy father, said Zenobia in a voice of enquiry, waving her hand for him to be seated.—And didst thou think I would ever quit thee? asked

Theodosius: no; I quit thee not, until the deaconess hath immersed thee in the waters of baptism, and thou art proclaimed to these regions a Christian.—The church waits, and I am come to receive thee; the baptizer is ready, be baptized, and to thy name of Zenobia add that of Augusta, at once comprehensive of thy dignity and having embraced a new religion. Perceiving that Zenobia turned her eyes upon the astonished Septimia as if to be guided thereby, he added, In political affairs, thou dost not here seek advice, refrain then in those of faith, for at thy time of life, O queen, reason hath arrived at full maturity, and it is now many years since thou hast governed this empire, guided alone by thy ripe and unassisted judgment.

This is all most wonderful, most mysterious! exclaimed Septimia. I have heard thy name, holy man, for who has not? but till now never saw thee here; yet you seem not strangers to each other. —I have seen the patriarch twice, replied Zenobia; at our first interview, he appeared to me destitute of every worldly comfort—at the second, he refused the government of Antioch—And at the third, interrupted Theodosius, he promises never more to leave thee; from this hour death alone shall remove thee from my sight.—And should I banish thee, said Zenobia, haughtily.—There spoke the queen—O less of that, and more of the Christian; check that spirit, and in time, or thou wilt become another Valerian. Valerian began by banishing, and ended in persecuting—the church he had protected many years, he at length tormented; three years was the church of Christ afflicted by his order, and where is Valerian now?

Where he shall not long remain, replied Zenobia—in the power of Sapor; but *his* misfortune was the chance and fate of war.—The *chance and fate* of war! repeated Theodosius: hast thou also learned those phrases? thou, who in thy journey from Armenia with this thy mother, stopped upon the banks of the rivers whereon once stood Babylon and Nineveh, and repeated the predictions of Isaiah? Did those cities also fall by chance and the fate of war?—Septimia and Zenobia looked surprised, when he continued, Hadst thou, O queen, remained in obscurity, few had enquired into the circumstances of thy infancy and progress through life, but since thy advancement to power, every action and word of thine have been traced and registered.

The death of Belshazzar, the overthrow of Tyre, the desolation of Chaldea, all this was foretold, replied Zenobia, but the captivity of Valerian who could foretell?—I, said Theodosius, without being inspired by Him who inspired the prophets, I anticipated all. Whilst the Roman emperor was a friend to the Christian church, I was his friend—when he became its persecutor, I was one of those persecuted; whilst he protected us, I was his bosom counsellor—when he shared his confidence with Macrianus, I forsook him.

And who was Macrianus? enquired Septimia.—A wily Egyptian, who, with Satan's own craft, urged him to the eighth persecution, which lasted three years; and at the end of the third, Valerian, betrayed by this same Macrianus, was shown in chains through Persia: the Egyptian told him that neither himself nor empire would prosper, unless the Christian were destroyed; I warned him that on lifting his hand against the Christian, destruction would come upon himself and empire, but my warning was vain. I foretold that God would not much longer suffer his chosen to be the victims of Pagan cruelty, but was disbelieved and proscribed.—Wert thou saved by miracle? asked Zenobia.—No, answered Theodosius, sternly, as he rebuked the sarcastic look and meaning of her words; not by miracle, but by the hand of Providence: I got on board a vessel bound to Gaza, and sailed for Jerusalem.

Odenathus, said Septimia, made more than one attempt to free the Roman emperor.—I know it, but can he be freed whose chains the hand of God doth rivet? Odenathus, invincible in every other cause, was ever baffled where the freedom of Valerian was concerned. He and the queen overran Persia, entered its capital, had almost their hands upon him, when news was brought that Palmyra was attacked; they both gave credit to the false report, and leaving Valerian to his fate, flew on the wings of duty to save Palmyra; yet never in their absence had a hand been lifted up against her, for Macrianus it was who spread the report: thus the man who urged Valerian to persecute the Christian, was made in the hand of God, the instrument of his punishment.

Zenobia considered, and with emotion

repeated the observation of Odenathus thereon—' The hand of heaven itself for some hidden purpose is surely against Valerian.' May I be more fortunate than was my husband! I have written to Sapor now in Media, and hourly expect the return of the messengers: no crowned head should sleep in peace while a brother sovereign mourns. I have implored his freedom, offered treasures inestimable, and the liberation of every Persian in my empire free of ransom; and if the answer be not satisfactory, my kingdom pours forth its population to his rescue.—And can the population of thy kingdom prevail over the will of the Almighty? asked the patriarch. To me the doom of Valerian appears irrevocable.

Zenobia, rising angrily, replied, I will not turn my face from the East until he is freed; they dare not attempt his life, for on me and Rome depend the lives of many thousand Persian slaves and captives, hostages for his safety: to my arms, and mine alone, shall be given the glory of redeeming Rome's emperor from captivity.

Her rising being the signal for Theodosius to depart, he also arose, when Longinus appeared with the messengers who were that instant arrived from Persia; the foremost held an open paper, which not daring to present to the queen, he gave Longinus.—It was not given thee thus? said Zenobia, alarmed.—Even thus, O mighty queen.—She turned to Longinus, and saw upon his face the pale hue of dismay as he slowly perused the letter from Sapor. Is this true? he asked.—Most true, they replied; our eyes saw it. Arrived at Ecbatana, we delivered our presents to the chief officer of the satraps, as he sat in the Syrian gate of the palace; he left us to seek the king, who was gone to review a newly-raised army of boys: almost immediately he returned, saying, Follow us; we did, and were led to the great fire-temple, where we will amply detail to thee all that met our eyes.—No, interrupted Longinus, and pointed to the door; the messengers obeyed the sign, and quitted the room. Addressing the queen, Longinus continued, Ere the receipt of thy letter, Sapor had received a threatening denunciation from Aurelian, and the consequence was immediate—Valerian is flayed alive.

Zenobia sank upon her couch, her head resting on the back thereof, her face concealed. Longinus, followed by Septimia and her grandson, left the presence, when Theodosius resumed his seat.

The first words of Zenobia on recovering this sudden and dreadful shock—Three months, and Ecbatana shall not have one stone upon another.—Three months, said the patriarch, calmly, and Palmyra may not have one stone upon another.—And when Palmyra shall be thus, retorted the queen, with dignity approaching to fierceness, where shall I be?

Thou! said Theodosius, tenderly, where wilt thou be, Zenobia! Though all mankind forsake thee, yet will not I: though deprived of empire, parents, children, friends, liberty, almost of life, I will never quit thee; standing by thy couch of misery and death, I will take my place to whisper comfort and salvation.

And this then is the fate of Valerian! sighed Zenobia, mournfully and in tears; greater than even mine was the empire of Valerian, and glorious was his reign, until, as thou hast made it appear, he became the enemy of Jesus Christ. Yet, O Theodosius, though I may adhere to the faith in which I was nurtured, do not fear me—I will not persecute; as hitherto, the Christian shall still throughout my realm meet assistance and protection.—It is not enough, replied the patriarch; more is expected of thee. I failed in my attempt to convert the aged Roman emperor, who, too deeply prejudiced in favour of the national polytheism, thought he did more than his duty in tolerating any other religion; but thou, the true believer in one God, the follower of the Mosaic law, who lookest for the coming of Messiah—thou, deeply read in controversy, skilled in various languages, if not converted, where will be thy excuse.

The mighty as thou seest are fallen; it is easy to fall—all things earthly are prone to fall; ten thousand fathoms we can plunge, but not rise a step without a sure foundation, a helping hand, a something to cling to—Oh, cling to this, (and he laid the scriptures on the table)— stretch forth thy hand to meet the hand divine stretched out to thee; be these the foundation of thy empire—on this rock be Palmyra built.

Zenobia looked towards a pile of books and rolls on an adjacent table, which look Theodosius understanding, selected several from among them, and brought and laid them before her. Hast thou, as I advised, compared this Latin translation of the Bible with the Syrian, the Syrian with the Hebrew, and that again with the Septuagint? Dost comprehend the wilful error made in chronology by those of thy faith, in order to prove that the Messiah is yet to come? But say, at what period of the world is he by thee expected?—At the end of four thousand years, replied Zenobia.— From the creation to the giving of the law, two thousand, and two other thousand from the giving of the law to the coming of Christ.—And how many years have elapsed since the creation?—Four thousand two hundred and seventy-one, answered Zenobia.—And two hundred and seventy-one years are elapsed, returned Theodosius, since the birth of Jesus Christ; thus was he born in the four thousandth year of the world. But, setting chronology aside, do not facts speak? At what period in thy political government was Shiloh (the Messiah) to come?—When the sceptre should depart from the hand of Judah.—And when did thy nation cease to be a nation?—At the death of the Maccabees, replied Zenobia, when Herod, an Idumenean, a descendant of Esau, became master of Judea and the posterity of Jacob; and thus was Isaac's prophecy fulfilled—'Thou shalt break thy brother's yoke from off thy neck, and shalt get the dominion.'—And in the reign of that same Herod, Christ was born, said the patriarch. Thus, by thy own confession, the sceptre had departed from Judah, and the priesthood from Levi: they exercised those functions but till the coming of Messiah; and Messiah then did appear to govern in his own person, to restore the Jewish theocracy—King of kings and Priest of priests.

If thou wouldst gain thy wish, observed the queen, I pray thee avoid all theological arguments, all subtle cavil and controversy; be simple in thy discourse to me, as Odenathus on a like occasion remarked, as if discoursing with a child. Thou hast not undertaken the conversion of a scholar, a learned disputant, but a female: and believe me, holy father, our judgment is seldom profound; we err more from weakness of mind than corruption of heart—our imagination is ardent and feeling acute, wherefore sensibility too often triumphs over reason. Although firmly convinced of all thou sayest, yet be aware that one look of my mother may for ever banish conviction.

And darest thou then, said the patriarch, thus meditate an excuse for future apostacy? Thou canst no more deceive me than thou canst thyself: thou art neither diffident as to the powers of thy mind or the acquired advantages of learning, and daily do pride and ambition grow upon thy nature; if in heart a Christian, in practice a Jewess, take heed of the judgment, and from this hour rather cultivate humility than affect it, for humility is the foundation of our faith. St. Paul was not lifted up into heaven to be convinced that the Jesus whom he considered it his duty to persecute was God; he was hurled to the earth, stricken blind, laid prostrate, in the dust. The truest symbol of united judgment, strength, swiftness, nobleness, and grace, is an armed man on horseback; St. Paul was thus, and well escorted: thus mounted, thus attended, he might have cut his way through an hostile army, but overtaken by a voice from heaven, the voice of Jesus, he fell nerveless as a new-born babe.

Zenobia wholly abashed and subdued by the rebuke of Theodosius, now indeed listened with unfeigned attention and meekness to him, whom she found no artifice could deceive, no majesty intimidate; and yet, though his eye was fire, his features never lost their sweet expression, or his voice its paternal softness.

Had I lived at that period, she observed, I had believed, but now——No, Zenobia: though cotemporary with the Saviour of man, thou mightest have been with others equally credulous.—We have no just conception of his person, remarked the queen.—Tradition, replied he, can give us but uncertain views of this particular; this we know, that by condescending to take our nature, he hath illustrated all its duties, and left a bright and perfect pattern of them for our perpetual example.—But, said Zenobia, if thou couldst conceive how painful is the idea of no longer looking forward to a Messiah, great, glorious, and powerful!—We Christians look forward to the same, replied Theodosius. Thou wonderest; it is not his *coming* we expect, but his *return* to judge both the quick and the dead: and yet indulging thy own hopes, I repeat to thee, Christ fulfilled those hopes, for he was great, and powerful, and glorious.—A marvellous contradiction! yet lowly born, humble, poor, and despised.—Could he have otherwise, asked the patriarch, have preached patience and temperance, peace and humility? What was the remark made to thee a few days back, by the voice of merited reproach—A queen cannot judge the feelings of a famished labourer?—Can he be styled lowly born, who was descended of the race of the royal David?—His occupation was humble, and therein he submitted in his own person to the sentence himself passed on Adam—' By the sweat of thy brow thou shalt earn thy bread.' Thus was labour neither impracticable nor degrading, for he stooped to labour; and yet though humble, more powerful was he than any earthly king. Did Augustus Cæsar ever feed thousands miraculously? Did Alexander restore life to his friend? Could Cyrus give sight to the blind? Or was the Persian monarch obeyed when he bade the elements be calm? A fishing-boat was at hand, or could Xerxes have walked from Europe to Asia upon the sea?

Moses, Elijah, Elisha, and others, also performed wondrous miracles, said Zenobia.—And by whose power?—The power of God, she replied.—And am I not preaching to thee that God, that same God, in whom we both believe? the God who made this world, who sentenced Adam, deluged the earth, conversed with the patriarchs, gave the law to Moses, and inspired the prophets: who anointed David king; sent Israel captive, gave Judah to Babylon, and restored Jerusalem: the God who descended from heaven, was worshipped in the flesh at Bethlehem, enlightened the doctors, compleated his ministry, died on the cross, rose from the sealed sepulchre, and ascended visibly into heaven: This is the God I come to preach.

Thus, said Zenobia, thou explainest Immanuel, God with us.—Even so; Immanuel, an embodied spirit.—Are we not all such?—No; the spirit of the Lord knew its previous state of being, and its future state. We are only conscious of present existence, and but for revelation, would be dark as to an hereafter.—And the first step to the throne of salvation is that of baptism? enquired Zenobia.

And thine, replied Theodosius, must be publicly acknowledged, not stealing into Christ's church, but boldly entering, and inviting followers; from that moment thou art emancipated — no longer the abject law-enslaved Jewess, but the free and pardoned Christian. Ask then in the name of Jesus Christ, receive and keep holy that name, and look for his return to judge the world; place thy people and thyself under his protection, and if thy prayer be granted, give him the glory.

On his again urging ere they separated, the necessity of speedy baptism, with real humility she asked what was previously required of her.—To believe in the great truths set forth in the public symbol of our common creed: to profess thyself a disciple of Christ, and to join in communion with his chosen, and so celebrate the benefits received by his death in the manner which he prescribed. A due period being then set for further conference, instruction, prayer, and meditation, the seal of baptism shall be withheld no longer.

Palmyra! chosen city of the East! blessed spot on which the dove of heaven hath descended! happy thou to be so blessed, so chosen! Look up, Palmyra, look to the Author of thy felicity; open thy ears to his voice, calling on thee to believe and obey. Scattered on a sunny hill (a stranger flock), ye browze and sleep, basking in luxurious security, yet as evening draws nigh, O hearken to the voice which saith, Hither, ye innocents, hither to me—come all of ye, come into my fold, and join the flock here assembled; rest in safety, whilst I keep watch. They hear the voice, yet few believe, and fewer still obey: some, stretched at their length, raise slowly the eye, and after a half-closed look of indifference, again lay it down, stretch every limb with voluptuous languor, and sleep again; others, affecting not to hear, move not, but continue chewing the juicy grass, whilst others, to escape the repeated call, rise and browze the contrary way, down, far down into the valley. The sun quits the hills, it quits the horizon, and the hour of security is over; the tiger and tigress, leaving their den, snuff the air, and take counsel together whither they shall go to fetch food for their whelps.

Cornelius, the centurion, though first a Pagan, became a ready convert to truth, for on embracing Judaism, it taught him a perfect knowledge of the holy scriptures; St. Peter but spake, and Cornelius was a Christian. No angel thus visibly prepared the way for Theodosius, yet Zenobia partly believed; and could Zenobia be long of one faith and Septimia of another? A month had not elapsed ere Septimia became almost the convert of the patriarch; she confessed that in time she might believe, and would no more. From day to day Zenobia also deferred baptism, and until her mother would consent to be baptized, refused to make a public declaration of her new faith.

Here my power ends, said the patriarch; to instruct, expound, exhort, implore, and correct, my duty enjoins—that fulfilled, I resign you to your own judgment: yet when I beheld the queen this morning enter our church, it was natural to expect her mother at her side.—Hast thou attended a Christian church? enquired Septimia.—I have, my mother, but not publicly. And, O holy father, how differently didst thou appear when amongst thy brethren, and when expounding truth to us! There thy discourse was calm, thy voice soft, thy looks serene, thy gesture unimpassioned. How truly paternal thy whole demeanour! But with us, though ever gracious, thy energy, thy enthusiasm makes our hearts—*my* heart, burn with equal fervour.

My duty there, said Theodosius, is only to confirm—here to convert. I have only to remind my brethren to be constant to their religious and moral obligations—my task here is to change the heart, to catch the kindled spark, and blow it to a flame. Among us no objection remains to be started, no question is expected, no answer is prepared—

here, do I not encourage thy mother to start every objection, propose every doubt, and endeavour to throw light upon obscurity.—With Christians the passions of the human breast must be kept undisturbed, with proselytes roused to exertion.

Christianity cannot be expected to spread with equal success through the Hebrew as through the Gentile world, remarked Septimia, their pagan religion, being from its nature, revolting to sense and reason, whilst ours was the gift of God himself.—It was, said Theodosius, and thereby is established the divinity of Christian revelation: in converting a Gentile we seek, point out, and expound the prophecies concerning the Messiah; but to a Hebrew we say, Recollect what say Moses and the prophets.

Moses doth not mention Christ by name, remarked Septimia. — The Israelites, replied Theodosius, who looked upon the brazen serpent lifted up on high, were healed and lived; all who look to Christ lifted up upon the cross and believe in him have everlasting life; wilt thou not profit by his death, Septimia? the death of him, at once the God and King of Israel?—Of Israel! exclaimed Septimia.—Yea, verily; was he not an Israelite, and descended from Abraham, Isaac, Jacob, Judah? had his descent been otherwise, he could not have been Messiah—oh, would but the Hebrew reflect, how exalted their nation over those of the Gentiles; thus their tribe, their country, to give birth to the Sovereign of the universe.—Is not every Jewish hope therein fulfilled, every promise made to them accomplished? Would it but acknowledge Christ, is it not the most favoured people on earth: thus to produce a king who will subject, or in other words convert, the whole Pagan world to his government and worship?— He came into his own kingdom and his own knew him not; him they adored invisible in the temple of Solomon, came suddenly to all in that of Zerubbabel. The tenacious Jews persisted still to watch the Holy of Holies, whilst their God was walking in the porch.

Septimia remarked, I have gone through the four gospels, and most diligently, but say, Theodosius, why did not St. Peter also write a gospel; a disciple who must have been most intimately acquainted with every particular of the life of Jesus Christ, from his own call to the death of his master—He did, said the patriarch.—And is it no longer extant? enquired Zenobia, if not I regret it: for methinks, such must have been more interesting than even these; the great simplicity, the candour yet timidity of his character, ennobled after the resurrection by such an extraordinary effusion of zeal and courage, must have rendered a narrative from him truly admirable and correct.

Thus, said Theodosius, hast thou passed a high eulogium upon the gospel I this morning read thee; the Gospel of St. Mark is the Gospel of St. Peter.—As the letters thou dictatest to Longinus are thine, not his, so is that gospel St. Peter's not St. Mark's; who only wrote down what his master dictated.—Neither is the gospel which goes under the name of St. Luke, the work of that Evangelist, but that of St. Paul, the firmest champion of christianity.—St. Matthew, one of the earliest disciples of our Lord, wrote in his own name, and St. John having examined the three, confirmed the truth of all, by writing the fourth.

A long pause ensued, broken at length by Zenobia: Wilt thou Theodosius be bishop, or rather patriarch of Syria?— No; he replied, I will not accept at thy hand, from a thread to a shoe latchet; I dwell among my brethren; no golden chain should be laid on lips inspired to preach the gospel; I will not be other than thy equal; for thou possessing all things, and I wanting nothing, we are on an equality; I have taken the conversion of thy soul upon me, and am now its guardian, and the guardian of thousands

I trust to be converted through thy means.

But having resigned that of Jerusalem, wilt thou not accept a revenue at my hands? — And what revenue dost think I enjoyed at Jerusalem?—Thy name was much renowned, replied Zenobia, and thy power over the church great and extensive, but having Paulus of Antioch, in idea, never can I divest the name of bishop from the grandeur and worldly magnificence which ever attends him.

Thou art from Calvary, remarked Septimia, hast thou left friends there, relatives; thou hast no family, holy father, hast thou? Were my family still in existence, he replied mournfully, I had not been here, as it had then been my duty to stay in the bosom of that family: At the foot of Mount Olivet lie buried my wife and three children; none remain to me; the last aged eighteen was laid in the grave a few days before I began my mission to Palmyra.— And what is the present state of Jerusalem? enquired Zenobia, eager to call off his attention from domestic sorrows, various and contradictory are the accounts I have received concerning it.—Come and behold, replied Theodosius, not from false zeal, but allowable curiosity: God is as much present where we now stand as at Jerusalem, but there is something greatly interesting in witnessing places where, when on earth he sojourned, where he was born and where suffered. This year is fixed for thy visit to Egypt, instead of a rapid flight through Judea thither, travel leisurely, and, guided by me, visit each holy spot in that sacred land. Many years back thou quittedst Armenia for a like purpose; thou wert then to have been led by the hand of an Israelite; heaven at that hour prevented thee, that thou mightst at this, go under the guidance of a Christian.

END OF THE EIGHTH BOOK.

ZENOBIA,

QUEEN OF PALMYRA

BOOK IX.

ARGUMENT.

Preparations for the royal journey to Judea—Omar the Arab takes charge of the young princes—Balbec—Damascus—Mount Lebanon—Sidon—Tyre—The lake of Tiberias—Capernaum—Zenobia's sorrowful reflections—She is encouraged by Theodosius—Nazareth—Mount Tabor—The hills of Gilboa—Jezreel—Cesarea—Samaria—Shiloh—Joppa—Idumea—The Red Sea—Bethlehem—Jerusalem—Mount Calvary—Theodosius blesses Zenobia, and his Christian flock assembled on the Mount of Olives.

Go forth ye messengers of glad tidings, go spread the word to the south that the queen cometh! Arm ye pioneers, and prepare the way, strike down the thorn, cut through the hill, and pick out the serpents from the clefts in the narrow passage of the rocks, strew bridges over marshy land, melt with fire the snow-topped mountain over which is thrown her road, and make the path hard for the chariot wheel, the army cometh on to scour away the enemy, the sumpter camels go forward to get ready the well-furnished tent, all things are prepared, all perils are done away, but nor pioneer, nor messenger, nor army, can intimidate or subdue the Arab.

On the morning of their departure Caleb, to whom the commission had been entrusted, appeared leading forward an Arab of the desert, whom he had engaged to protect them through Upper Syria and Arabia—Oh, it is wild Ishmael himself! exclaimed Timolaus, shrinking fearfully away and hiding behind his brother.—Timolaus, said Zenobia, come forward.—He obeyed.—Do thou and Herennianus, go and take Omar the Arab by the hand, salute that hand and put it to your forehead.—This ceremony, so dreadful to the boys performed, they would again have retired, when Omar, seizing them in his arms, ran and placed them on camels held in attendance by a guide: he put the bridles in one hand, and ivory rods in the other, and regardless of every other person, appeared to devote his whole soul to the children thus given to his protection.

The princes are secure from harm through the remainder of this journey, remarked Caleb turning away, while Septimia expressed her fears that the Arab would steal them. It had been the wish of Septimia to accompany Zenobia in this expedition, but infirmity rendered it unsafe and at the request of her husband and daughter, she consented to remain in Palmyra with the younger child Vaballathus. I leave these books with thee, said Theodosius at parting, make use of them, study the Scriptures when thou art alone, but read not the works of our Christian fathers without him, whom I have appointed to attend thee for that purpose; Irenius, our pastor of this place, will select such passages as are fitting thy perusal, wherefore confide in his judgment, and at my return may I, through the grace of God, number thee a member of the church

Preceded, flanked and followed by armies, the queen and her sons quitted Palmyra, and began their journey attended by Theodosius, Victorinus, and other nobles, together with several women, among whom were Victoria (whose husband Claudian, being gone to Rome, she consented to accompany Zenobia), and Terentia, the widow of Marcus Terentius, the most favoured and beloved of all her female train. They crossed the Orontes and long halted on its myrtle banks, then repaired to Balbec, where Zenobia, for the first time, visited the temple, in which was pronounced the former oracle concerning herself. The architecture of this city almost equals that of Palmyra, remarked Zenobia, so rich its sculptured walls, gigantic piles,

Corinthian wreaths, and well carved eagles; perhaps, in the judgment of some, surpasses it; but I would not exchange my capital for this: say, Theodosius, will Balbec outlive my Palmyra? —I am no prophet, he replied, but of this be convinced, the gospel hath not yet been preached there.

On arriving at Damascus, the youths were enchanted at the paradise around them, its fountains, gardens, vineyards, and orchards, called forth all their admiration, but to that was added, the deepest interest when Theodosius informed them, that here had our first parents settled at their expulsion from Eden, and pointed out the tomb of Abel: to Zenobia he shewed the house of Annanias, whither St. Paul was taken, and half a mile from the east gate of the city the spot where he was stricken by heaven to the earth, when pursuing his mad career of persecution.

Zenobia travelled in silence, interested and amused by the incessant questions of her sons, who suffered nothing to escape their notice, and those around them were strictly charged to satisfy every enquiry, whilst Omar, who seemed to think them youthful gods dropped from heaven, watched every look, and listened to every word with intent earnestness, that he might anticipate their expression of a wish. Arrived on the summit of Lebanon, where slumbers everlasting snow, a glorious prospect presented itself: the rich valley of Balbec, the flat desert stretching to the Persian Gulf, the whole land of Judea, and the Mediterranean Sea; but soon the prospect became obscured, clouds gathered beneath their feet, lightning darted, and thunder burst far below. Timolaus, as he looked down from the edge of a precipice, turned pale and put his hand before his eyes, saying to his brother, who shewed no signs of fear—never can we descend through this! Omar heard the words, and darting upon the timid boy, wrapped him closely from head to foot in his own ample cloak: then uttering a species of wild song, that he designed should encourage and exhilarate, he rushed down the mountains, leaping from crag to crag, winding through paths hardly accessible to the goat, and disappeared among the clouds beneath. Zenobia and her train, after a tedious journey, also reached the southern plains, and, there seated on a sunny hillock, they beheld Timolaus eating a newly gathered shaddock, and Omar, half-stretched on the ground, watching beside him.

By how many names hath this, our new acquisition been known? asked Herennianus.—By six, replied Zenobia; the land of Canaan from the sons of Canaan, the grandson of Noah, having possessed themselves of it; it was in truth the patrimony of Shem, for after the deluge, the world being the gift of God to Noah, he alone had the sole privilege of bequeathing it at pleasure· the same as a private individual bequeaths his personal estate, he gave this land to Shem, whose descendants, in after ages, under Joshua, expelled the usurping and idolatrous posterity of Ham.—To Abraham, of the family of Shem, it was therefore promised and called in consequence the Land of Promise. Abraham was blessed by Shem or Melchisedeck, who, born in the old world, of no generation was he in the new world; therefore figuratively without father or mother.—Melchizedeck, king of Salem and the priest of the High God, surrounded by usurpation and paganism, confirmed the promise to Abraham, that the land should be yet restored to the rightful owner. When divided into two kingdoms, it was named the land of Judah and Israel; and when Israel went into captivity, it was known by the superior title of Judea. The Philistines on the sea coast who were never wholly dispossessed, gave it the name of Palestine, and it is now by Christians justly called the Holy Land.

And what is its extent? asked Timolaus.—The extent of the Lesser Canaan, replied Zenobia, from Dan to Beersheba is a hundred and forty miles, and from Jordan to the Mediterranean fifty; the Greater Canaan extended from Mount Lebanon to the shores of the Red Sea, and from the Mediterranean to the Euphrates—thus was the promise made to Abraham nobly fulfilled: 'Unto thy posterity have I given this land from the river of Egypt unto the great river Euphrates;' and of this land, his descendant Solomon, of the fourteenth generation, was king; who, while he continued faithful to God, was blessed of God: for in riches and wisdom he exceeded all the kings of the earth.

Solomon possessed his kingdom in peace? enquired the elder boy doubtingly.—He did; and thus was ensured the building and dedication of the temple, but the sins of the fathers were visited on the children; ten tribes revolted to Jeroboam and formed themselves into a kingdom named Israel, those remaining, Judah and Benjamin, alone continuing faithful to Rehoboam the son of Solomon.—But Israel, said Timolaus, did not long prosper.—No; rebellion and ingratitude never can; their chusing of their own accord an obscure subject, in defiance of him, who, though weakly led astray, was still their king and the son of David, anointed by God himself, brought down ruin upon them; the Assyrian, Shalmanazer, was sent against them, and ten tribes were taken captive.—Methinks, remarked Herennianus, that this had been sufficient warning to the kingdom of Judah to avoid idolatry.—Most true, replied his mother, yet, despising that sacred warning, they persisted in offence, and Nebuchadnezzar was made the instrument of divine vengeance; the eyes of Zedekiah, their last king, were put out, and they suffered a captivity of seventy years.

'By the waters of Babylon we sat down and wept,' repeated Timolaus, and Cyrus at the end of that period permitted them to return and rebuild the walls and the temple; but, my mother, are there no remains of the ten dispersed tribes?—Yes; for it was spoken by the same voice which doomed them to captivity, that a remnant should be saved.—Of what tribe are we? asked the elder.—Septimia is of the tribe of Benjamin, her forefathers were taken captives to Babylon, and at the destruction of that city, their descendants were transplanted to Seleucia on the Euphrates, where was born my mother and thy uncle Elkanah.

But in the time of Augustus Cæsar, when this land was a Roman province, it was distinguished by other appellations.—True, replied Zenobia; Herod the Great being dead, his kingdom was divided among his sons, yet still under Roman jurisdiction. Galilee, on which we are entering, was peopled by a remnant of the ten tribes, Samaria adjoining was colonized by Medes and Persians, and Judea to the south became the real habitation of the tribes of Judah and Benjamin, wherefore both Samaria and Galilee were ever held in hatred and contempt by the Jews, (the inhabitants of Judea) and Jerusalem its capital.

On quitting Lebanon, Omar, whose attention was ever fixed on the youths, perceiving Herennianus grow pale and languid with intense heat, he led his camel to the shade of a rock, and fetched him one of the leather bottles from the carrier, but the boy finding the water heated and unpalatable put it gently from him, Omar raising it to his own lips understood the cause, when, pouring it upon the sand, he disappeared. Zenobia and her company had reached the spot where lay Herennianus, when the Arab returned, swift as the wild roe of the mountains, with the water-skin filled to the brim: he held it to the prince, who quaffed the cool refreshing stream, and returned it to Omar, the remainder he drank himself, and directing the company to proceed on their way, sat down in the shade at the foot of the rock, and taking the head of the child made it repose on his shoulder. Oppressed with heat and fatigue, Herennianus closed his eyes, and when he again opened them, the heats were past away, the moon lightened the smiling prospect, and he breathed new life: but he was not longer suffered to indulge in rest; the Arab caught him in his arms, and bounding forward, overtook the queen near the fountain from whence he had fetched the water, the springs Jor and Dan, from which the sacred river flowed.

Entering Phœnicia, they proceeded straightway to Sidon, its capital, the mother of Tyre, and there what subject for meditation on fallen human grandeur! Sidon, once the proud and magnificent, the seat of arts and learning! Theodosius was received with due honours, and entering the Christian church, there officiated. Passing the east gate, he approached Zenobia, whose wish for a private reception having been made known, was duly respected, and addressed her—On the spot where now we stand, said he, knelt the woman of Canaan, when importunately beseeching the Saviour of man to heal her daughter, his reply was, 'Great is thy faith, be it done unto thee as thou wilt.' Was not this the literal accomplishment of these words—'Ask, and it shall be given—knock, and it shall be opened?' I, Zenobia, in my own person can truly declare, I never yet asked and was refused, without being subsequently convinced that the refusal was a blessing.— The look of the queen seemed to answer, Because all thy desires are pure and holy.

On looking back at Sidon, Do not, asked Theodosius, do not the prophecies of Isaiah, Ezekiel, and Jeremiah, present themselves to thy mind? those prophecies foretelling its destruction, and which, under Ochus, King of Persia, were so awfully fulfilled?—Zenobia was silent, an air of melancholy came over her countenance, and though the predictions were trembling on her tongue, her heart refused to give them utterance.

When in sight of Sarepta, The barrel

of meal shall not waste, exclaimed Timolaus, neither shall the cruize of oil fail, until the Lord send rain upon the earth. O should I die young, that there were an Elijah to restore me to my widowed mother!—An affectionate look was all the answer made by Zenobia; her heart was full.

Arrived at Tyre, her silence and dejection were noticed by all; no prophecy, no comment was repeated or made. She checked her camel when crossing a wide and desolated plain overspread for nineteen miles around with splendid ruins, and looked upon the neighbouring town: Theodosius continued at her side; he read all that passed in her mind, and though she still refused to make it known, now shewed he already knew all.

O Tyre! impurpled, golden Tyre! he said, once the proudest, most princely city of the earth! thou that rejoiced in the fall of Jerusalem! ' Behold, I am against thee, said the Lord; nations shall destroy thy walls, O Tyre, and break down thy towers, scrape off thy dust, and make thee like the top of a rock, a place for fishers to dry their nets on. I will bring upon Tyre, Babylon from the north with horses and chariots, and he shall break down thy walls and enter thy gates, and slay thy people by the sword, and thou shalt no more be built, said the Lord God.'

But it was rebuilt, replied Herennianus, and afterwards destroyed by Alexander.—No, my child, said Zenobia, mournfully, it never was: the prophecy repeated by Theodosius refers to antient Tyre, of which this desolated spot on the continent is the site, and these its splendid ruins; here reigned Hiram, cotemporary with Solomon. The Tyre which Alexander destroyed, was built on yonder spot, then an island joined by him to the continent, and the third Tyre is, as thou seest, situated on the peninsula thus formed.—Then still, replied Timolaus, Tyre exists, though not in situation, in name, and the prophecy is not yet completely fulfilled.—The completion, my child, returned Theodosius, is not averted, but delayed. Times are in the hand of the Lord, and ages may pass away ere the fulfilment of this shall be witnessed by man, but the time will surely come when the traveller shall bear witness against it: he shall here seek, and find no nation; standing on a ruined sandy shore, he shall not even see the remains of yon stately city now before our eyes, he shall not find one stone upon another, but shall distinguish its sole inhabitants, five fishermen, abiding on the top of a rock, hanging their nets to dry thereon.

They quitted the coast, and travelled eastward to the sea of Galilee. To Timolaus' enquiry, Zenobia answered, that it was also distinguished by the names of Chinnereth, Gennesareth, and Tiberias; that it was in length a hundred furlongs, and in breadth forty.— This, remarked the patriarch, as they stood upon its borders, is the only sea on which our Saviour embarked, and here were performed many of his miracles.

As all things appertain to the Lord, said the queen, why have solicited what was already his? why, instead of saying, 'Go out, I pray thee, a little from land,' did he not enter the ship of his own will, and miraculously put to sea?—To set an example of respect to property, yet instantly he performed the miracle of the draught of fishes, as to reward their hospitable and gracious compliance: he walked on the sea, therefore had no need of human inventions; his design in entering ships, we may suppose, to manifest his approbation of science and industry. As man, he deigned to feed with man: when human means failed in procuring a supply, he, as God, supernaturally fed thousands; as man, he sought food upon the fig-tree — as Jehovah, he cursed it.— Could not the tongue which said, Be withered, have also said, Be hung with fruit?—He amply supplied the wants o others, yet himself practised self-denial · when in the wilderness forty days and forty nights, human aid was out of reach, his angels ministered to him; given over to extremity of distress, and hope in man is lost, heaven is ever near at hand.

Is the age of miracles gone by? enquired Zenobia.—It is: have faith, but expect no miracles, and to faith add self-exertion; faith alone produces nothing—joined to exertion, all things. Behold yon plant on the ground; should I look at it, saying, I believe that in time the earth may cover that plant, the rain hollow it a bed, and it strike root, what do I but tempt God? Is it not my duty, if I wish it to grow, to put it myself in the ground? Natural causes may prevent its growth, but my part is done, and for the rest I pray for the blessing of God on it, and believe that he will hear my prayer.

What towns do we now approach? asked the queen. And why delay our progress towards Nazareth?—First, visit north of this sea, three places remarkable for having incurred the malediction of the Lord, said the patriarch, impressively. 'Woe to thee, Chorazin! woe unto thee, Bethsaida! And thou, Capernaum, which art exalted unto heaven, shalt be brought down to hell, for if the mighty works done in you had been done in Tyre and Sidon, they would have repented long ago in sackcloth and ashes.' Here, at Bethsaida, were born three of the apostles, Peter, Philip, and Andrew, and here Jesus gave sight to the blind. At Capernaum, how great, how numerous the miracles there performed, and every miracle a blessing! There the centurion asked and obtained the life of his diseased servant, Jairus received the reanimated body of his daughter, the palsied was healed, and Peter's mother cured: the disciples, armed with power, in his name cured, but also inflicted death, and blindness, and other judgments; but Christ in his own person, was all goodness, mercy, and clemency.

On yonder eminence, near the coast, continued the patriarch, was given the discourse called the Sermon on the Mount Think of the perverse comments of the Jewish teachers on the law of Moses, and compare it with the commandments so full of grace and truth here delivered:—Not life for life, in their unqualified vindictive sense, eye for eye, nor tooth for tooth—burning for burning, wound for wound, nor stripe for stripe; but Blessed are the humble in spirit, they that mourn, the meek, the merciful, the pure in heart, the peacemaker Yet here he adds, Think not I come to destroy the law and the prophets, (for they allowed but public and judicial retributions, and even those much moderated and kept clear of private resentments;) I come not to destroy, but to fulfil. Love your enemies, do good to them that hate you, pray for them that persecute you.

Was it not here, asked Zenobia, where now we stand, that after this sermon, he embarked to cross over to the opposite coast, when overtaken by the tempest?—It was · 'The ship was covered with the waves, but he was asleep; his disciples woke him, saying, Lord, save us, we perish; and he rebuked the winds and the sea, and there was a great calm.' These disciples were fishermen, accustomed from youth to the dangers of the elements; how awful then this storm to inspire them with terror, and suspend exertion to escape it! Well practised in the natural changes of the elements, how truly convinced that this great and sudden calm was miraculous!

Zenobia listened, but with an air of unusual despondency. Are there not other storms than those of winds and waves? continued Theodosius; other dangers than those arising from sinking vessels? Thy bosom is wholly free from passion; the filial, conjugal, and maternal passion alone has ever visited that bosom; but there are others requiring constant watch to calm and subdue—ambition, injustice, cruelty, deceit: if ever agitated by such, O rush to the throne of thy Maker, and say, ' Lord, save, or I perish !' or if the victim of the crimes of others, thy kingdom threatened, thy person menaced, cling to the Saviour of the world, and he will arise, saying, ' Why art thou fearful, O thou of little faith ?' He will rebuke the threatening storm, he will guard thee from peril, and establish a blessed calm.

The queen, more offended at his suspicions than affected by his paternal remonstrance, coolly demanded, What is this dire calamity thou art ever predicting to myself and people? Of late, thy admonitions have daily taken this cheerless turn; what canst thou fear, what apprehend? ' Sufficient to the day is the evil thereof.'

O quote not the words of scripture in this thy untoward state of mind! I neither foresee nor have predicted any calamity either to thy realm or person: nay, far otherwise; to thee I look for the performance of the greatest, most glorious deed that hath ever been attempted —the perfect and universal conversion of the East, both Jew and Gentile. Mistake not the words of truth for those of adulation; praises from lips like mine are designed not to inspire vanity, but to raise the depressed spirit, and arm the mind with piety and fortitude. Thou art not ignorant of thyself; hear then from me the consciousness of thy perfection confirmed, that thou mayst not hereafter plead one excuse to palliate the slightest failure in the work thou wert born to perform. Highly favoured of heaven, by divine grace well prepared to receive the gospel, I but arrived, and it was received. Thus was gained one in whom determined resolution and masculine wisdom is joined extensive learning and commanding eloquence, with the softest, tenderest heart —a form which fills every heathen subject with adoration, and reminds the Hebrew of the awful and majestic beauty of a conquering Judith, blended with the attractive graces of a blushing Esther. Of thee it may be said, as of Capernaum, O Zenobia! which art exalted unto heaven —— Something, I know not what, has of late agitated thy mind. It is not anxiety as to the state of Palmyra in thy absence, since daily thou receivest letters from thy father of its welfare? If thou dost repent this journey, speak but the word, and we will go no further; fear not me—I will also relinquish it. Say, most honoured, shall we return to Palmyra?

Oh, holy father, pardon, O pardon! she replied, this deep dejection of spirits which I in vain endeavour to repress—a dejection that suddenly seized me when seated on one of the fallen columns among the ruins of Tyre. She stopped and hesitated, but encouraged by Theodosius, continued, When I reflect on what Tyre once was, the brilliant diamond in the golden crown of the world, and that my Palmyra owes its present greatness to the fall of Tyre and the destruction of

Jerusalem; when I think upon the changes that nations undergo, my heart at that moment——Oh, Theodosius! pity, but do not rebuke me—these boys are not dearer to me than is Palmyra.

Rebuke thee! said the patriarch, and he turned away his face.—My mother! exclaimed Timolaus, thou weepest! and he would have thrown his arms around her neck, had not his brother with tender respect drawn him silently away.

Zenobia, said Theodosius, with altered voice, hear me once again, and glory in being made an instrument in the hand of God. Having escaped the idle and voluptuous inactivity which religion and the climate imposes on the women of these parts, thou mayst look forward to thirty years of happy existence, and in that time what may not thy zeal and example effect? I repeat, thy presence alone ensures converts; point to the gospel, saying, ' This is my faith, be it yours,' and thou spreadest over these regions the kingdom of Jesus Christ. Be

Palmyra first converted, and abide religiously by the pure doctrines of the gospel, the Messiah will be its protector; let Palmyra give itself to him, and he will guard his own.

Zenobia reviving, attempted to smile, saying, Would that the age of prophecy had not ceased, and thou wert truly inspired when foreboding good to Palmyra! —And canst thou, O queen, doubt my words? On thy return, proclaim to thy empire that thou holdest Paganism in abhorrence, hast abjured Judaism, and will embrace Christianity, and mark the consequence:— heathen temples will sink into dust, oracles cease, human sacrifices end—the red-hot arms of Moloch will no more clasp the shrieking infant, the horrid sound of drums drowning the mother's screams, be no longer heard— amphitheatres will no more be crowded to witness blood and carnage, captive monarchs no more dragged in triumph at the conquerors' chariot-wheels, or prisoners of war massacred to appease the manes of the dead: man will no longer sell man—superfluous, cruel, and absurd ordinances will cease—with heathen temples will disappear, synagogues equally impious, and *thus* the Hebrew be *recalled* to reason, the kingdom of the Messiah be established, and wheresoever that blessed kingdom is settled in its first purity, asylums for old age will rise—hospitals for the diseased, the blind, the lame, be erected—funds established for the necessitous—houses of reform built for destitute penitents, and schools for their deserted offspring; all will be mercy, brotherhood, and charity: the cross will rise triumphant in the East, drawing after it the hearts of men; at the name of Jesus every knee shall bow, and all will bless the name of Zenobia.

Zenobia looked stedfastly at Theodosius, and almost could have exclaimed, with the council who gazed upon St. Stephen, 'His face is as the face of an angel.' She took his hand, and bowing over it, said, This is the hand that shall baptize me—this hand shall issue the decree for building churches in every province of my realm, and the Almighty do the rest: from that hour dejection fled her countenance.

As they remounted to proceed on their way, Zenobia enquired, Will Rome, thinkest thou, ever embrace Christianity? And should it, will uninterrupted prosperity be the consequence?—Such an event is most probable, replied the patriarch, for the memory of St. Paul is there still fresh and revered, and Christianity hath widely spread through Italy; but should hereafter a Roman emperor renounce Paganism, he must be aware that it is requisite to be a Christian in nature as well as name, an immoral Christian being farther from heaven than a virtuous Hebrew or a Pagan. On the posterity of Solomon the beloved and magnificent, fell the avenging scourge equally with the idolatrous Babylonian. Rome may be converted, may decline, and fall: the mere historian will record the facts of so momentous an event; had not the age of prophecy expired, inspiration, as in the case of Babylonia, Assyria, and the cities of Phœnicia, would relate the cause.

Zenobia, with renovated spirits, pursued her way, devoting her sole attention to Theodosius, for her sons, under the protection of Omar, a being who appeared possessed of powers more than human, was wholly divested of care on their account. Omar let them neither suffer heat, cold, hunger, thirst, nor weariness; he administered to their pleasures, joined in their sports when a halt longer than usual permitted it; and watched their sleep; amidst sterility they were supplied with abundance, and had only to express a wish for grapes, citrons, almonds, or other fruit, and it was ever supplied. O that that scarlet bird were mine! exclaimed the younger, and the flamingo was brought to him on the point of Omar's arrow. How noble, cried the other, to see the chace of the ostrich!—the ostrich, at the instant, was forced to begin its running flight, for Omar pursued it: turned every way it ran through the camp in circles, and until the princes gave signs for the chace to cease, the Arab never halted to take breath.

The night air having seized Timolaus, his faithful Omar disappeared with him, and the next morning restored the child to his mother free of disease. Omar, said Timolaus, took me to a field, and killed four sheep successively, and bathed my limbs in their warm blood. Herennianus riding his favourite Egyptian horse over a ground strewn with thorns and brambles, the beast stumbled; the boy applied the spur, and the horse became ungovernable: Would thou wert dead! exclaimed the angry youth, and the arm of the over-zealous Arab struck him dead on the spot. Instantly the air was filled with lamentation, and Herennianus overtaking his mother, complained of his loss. It was thy own desire, replied

Zenobia, calmly, therefore blame thyself; and he was left to follow on foot. He cast his eyes around, and on seeing a traveller pass, muttered, I wish thy camel were mine; the traveller was instantly dismounted by the Arab, who placed the boy on his back. Zenobia saw the transaction, and indemnified the stranger five-fold on his voluntarily relinquishing the camel; when turning to Victorinus, she remarked, And I could almost wish we were deprived of this dreadful minister of vengeance.

Behold the brow of yon steep hill, said the patriarch, there in a concave valley on its summit is Nazareth Nazareth, exclaimed Zenobia, where the infant Jesus was nurtured, brought up, and lived until he entered on his ministry? The same: where he became subject to his parents and encreased in stature and in wisdom, growing in favour with God and man. They ascended the hill and entered the town. Having visited the house of Joseph they repaired to the synagogue.—Here, said Theodosius, his baptism and temptation passed, Jesus came, and where, Zenobia, for sublimity and grandeur can be found a passage to equal the description of his entering on his ministry; read it thyself, in the same synagogue, at the same desk, with the same meek spirit.

'And he came to Nazareth, where he had been brought up, and as his custom was, went into the synagogue on the Sabbath-day, and he stood up to read, and there was delivered unto him the book of the prophet Isaiah, and when he had opened the book he found the place where it was written, 'The spirit of the Lord is upon me because he hath appointed me to preach the gospel to the poor; he hath sent me to heal the broken hearted, to preach deliverance to the captive, to give sight to the blind, to set at liberty them that are bruised, to preach the acceptable year of the Lord.' And he closed the book and gave it again to the minister and sat down, and the eyes of all that were in the synagogue were fastened on him, and he began to say unto them—This day is this scripture fulfilled in your ears.'

Yet his words were not believed, remarked Zenobia.—On our leaving the town, replied Theodosius, I will shew the brow of the hill, from whence they would violently have cast him down headlong; the divine nature then interposed, and as a shadow peradventure he escaped, for the words are—He passing through the midst of them went his way; and, but that he came into the world to suffer, could he not as easily in the garden of Gethsamene have passed away unhurt?

On crossing the valley of Esdralon, Zenobia perceived Theodosius contemplating a high mountain standing apart, of cone-like shape resembling none other. That is Mount Tabor, he replied, and thereon took place the transfiguration. Thus Elijah did verily come down from heaven, as witnessed by the apostles, before the coming of the dreadful day of wrath in which Jerusalem was overwhelmed. At every step hereafter thou wilt find the events recorded in the Old and New Testament mingled, but well read in each, confusion is easily avoided. We have passed Naim at the foot of Mount Hermon, where the widow's only son was raised to life (as easy to restore animation as at first to give it), the town of Endor, where Saul consulted the sorceress, and Bethulia; saved by Judith from the Assyrian Holofernes. Yonder, to the right is Shunem, now only a village, where lived the wealthy matron who provided a room for Elisha, and to whom Elisha said what kings could not —Be embraced by thy son, restored from the dead.

On the mountains of Gilboa they stopped to examine the place where Saul lost crown and life, and when standing thereon—' O Jonathan,' exclaimed the gentle Timolaus; ' I am distressed for thee, my brother Jonathan, the beauty of Israel is slain! how are the mighty fallen, and the weapons of war perished!" The arm of Timolaus as he spake was passed round the neck of Herennianus, on whom he leaned, and when he repeated, 'I am distressed for thee, my brother,' the emotion of Zenobia was narrowly observed by Theodosius.

We approach the royal city of Jezreel, said he, and shall stand on what was once the vineyard of Naboth—thou wilt see the spot where dogs devoured Jezabel, and that spot once red with the blood of Ahab: hast thou lately read, art well acquainted with the eighteenth chapter of the second book of Chronicles? Zenobia, struck with the peculiar solemnity of his manner, could not answer, and he continued, That chapter be thy future guide.—I recollect, said Zenobia, that Ahab, King of Israel, entered into a treaty of peace with Jehoshophat, King of Judah, and that, deceived by the united voices of four hundred false prophets, he went up against the King of Syria, and was slain at Ramoth Gilead

True, said Theodosius; Ahab, the worshipper of Baal, the husband of the idolatrous Sidonian Jezabel, the persecutor of the prophets of God, was yet, by the mercy of the Lord, warned of the event of that battle. The four hundred, in the spirit of flattery, said, Go up, for God will deliver Syria into thy hand. Micaiah, single among the wicked, said, in the spirit of truth, I see all Israel scattered upon the hills, as sheep that have no shepherd. Yet Ahab suffered this holy prophet to be stricken in his presence, and then commanded him to a prison.—A prison! repeated Zenobia, I remember not that circumstance.—Deaf to the prophetic voice, continued Theodosius, Ahab joined cruelty and injustice to impiety, and ordered *him* to captivity, the bread of affliction and the water of affliction, whose advice, had he followed, he had neither lost life nor kingdom—study this chapter, Zenobia, study it well, it is a lesson peculiarly adapted to sovereigns.

In their way to Cesarea, they passed the cave where Obadiah and the hundred prophets were concealed from Jezabel.—These subterraneous dwellings, remarked Theodosius, unknown to Palmyrene, are common to our Judea; in these deep recesses of the mountains, are chambers made by nature and improved by art, which, branching into others, could well contain whole armies.—Nay, while we speak, added Victorinus, though the entrance of yon cave appear desolate, may not there lurk beneath our feet a horde of Arabs.

I would not have the fidelity of our Arab, or the valour of our generals be put to trial, replied Zenobia, urging the pace of her camel; let us hasten therefore to Cesarea, that renowned city, beautified in' honour of Julius. On arriving at it, Here, said Theodosius, dwelt Cornelius, the first Gentile converted; here also dwelt Philip, the evangelist, and the prophet Agabus, who foretold the dearth in the reign of Claudius and the death of St. Paul; and we now enter the hall of judgment, where, on yonder throne, sat Herod Antipas, the royal sumptuous Herod, the persecutor of the church; this wide and splendid area was filled with idolaters, who, when Herod spake, shouted, ' It is the voice of a god, not of a man!' and at the same instant, this, their god, crowned and arrayed in purple, fell from his throne, stricken by disease and death. Hither was St. Paul sent prisoner, by Ananias the high priest, and accused by him and Tertullus before Felix the governor of that city, St. Paul pleaded the cause of Christianity.

I did not, answered Zenobia, say to thee, Go thy way for this time, when I have a convenient season I will call for thee.—thou receivedst me as the apostle of truth should ever be received, but let not presumption overshadow the brightness of a candid and unprejudiced mind. —The soul of Felix was dark, thine enjoyed faint twilight, fast emerging into sunshine.—Here, at this judgment seat, sat Agrippa and Bernice; and here, at the foot of the throne, stood St. Paul, not one of the twelve apostles yet as great, whose upright heart, known to that Jesus whom, not knowing, he persecuted, was, by that same Jesus, who descended purposely from heaven, converted to the knowledge of truth: his noble extraction, his learning, religious education, fervour, and piety, rendering him an invaluable instrument to spread the gospel through the Gentile world; and to the Hebrew, he said, In condemning Jesus,' you have yourselves fulfilled the prophets.

On quitting Cesarea, they visited Samaria, the former capital of the kings of Israel and the proud rival of Jerusalem. Here, said Theodosius, to please Herod, the daughter of Herodian danced, and yonder is the prison where, at her desire, the Baptist was beheaded. From the summit of this hill of Samaria, near yonder grove of tamarinds, is Dothan where Joseph was sold to the Midianites; and there the well where our Saviour said to the woman, 'I am Messiah.' Between the mountains Gerizim and Ebal, whereon the blessings and curses were pronounced, is Shechem, where Jacob dwelt.

Crossing to the Jordan, they saw where St. John baptized; they visited the wilderness of Bethabara and the house of Elizabeth the mother of John; wherein Mary gave praise to God, saying, 'My soul doth magnify the Lord, and my spirit hath rejoiced in God my Saviour'—the towering height of Mount Pisgah, from whence Moses viewed the Holy Land was pointed out to them; they saw Mount Nebo on which Moses died, and where the ark of the covenant was hid by the Maccabees; and then turning westward to Jericho, leaving Bethlehem and Jerusalem to be visited the last, they no longer journeyed forward with undeviating regularity, but resorted to each spot as curiosity dictated.—Shall we not see the palm of Deborah? enquired Timolaus.—Thou shalt, my son, replied Zenobia, thou shalt go thither, conducted by thy Arab, and beneath its shade where she judged Israel, sing the song of Deborah. And I to Bethel, where Jacob had his dream, said Herennianus.

We now approach Shiloh, observed Theodosius, where, when Canaan was conquered, the tabernacle was set up and remained four hundred years until the building of the temple: this was the residence of Samuel and Eli, the prophet and judge of Israel; Eli! sad example of an ill-judging parent, whose sinful neglect, in punishing his sons, lost him honour, life, and posterity.

From thence they passed to Rama, and again westward to the Mediterranean.—Here to Joppa fled the prophet Jonah, remarked the patriarch, designing to go to Tarsus, but the divine word said, 'Proceed to Nineveh,' and who shall resist that word unpunished? he was thrown into the raging sea, and the sea became calm;

how often are the brute creation made instruments to perform the will of the Maker of all!—The whale which swallowed Jonah, the ass which reproved Balaam, the lion that tore the rebellious prophet, those that spared Daniel, the bears which devoured the young men mockers of Elisha, the ravens by whom Elijah was fed, all the agents of him who said, ' a sparrow falls not to the ground unseen of me.'— At Joppa dwelt Dorcas the pious, raised to life by St. Peter, and six miles northward is Lydda, where Eneas was cured by that apostle of the palsy.

Methinks, said Herennianus, we are not far from Gath; I would see the birth place of Goliah the Philistine, and the sepulchre of Samson.—They went to both, and also to Gaza, the principal city of the Philistines, doomed to destruction, as foretold by the prophet Zephaniah, and razed to the earth by Alexander.

And now, remarked Theodosius, in our progress to Egypt we come to the south country, made interesting by the recollection of the patriarchs Abraham, Isaac, and Jacob, and which was ennobled by the residence of a Sarah and a Rebekah, we shall pass through the wilderness of Shur, where Hagar and Ishmael wandered in sorrow, and over the mountains of Paran, where Esau strung his bow.

Quitting the boundaries of Judea, the travellers entered on Arabia Petrea, and then was first experienced the protection of Omar. To every hovering band of Arabs, which appeared at intervals, he approached, and each successively disappeared. In their way to Mounts Sinai and Horeb they passed through an Arab camp, consisting of ten thousand tents and sixty thousand head of cattle. The women brought Zenobia stuffs of silk and gold and silver, or linen or cotton woven by their hands; and the men rice and barley and other corn, all of which she purchased at two-fold the price; she accepted from the hand of their chief a cup of curdled milk, and a cake dipped in the oil of dates, and gave them in return the flowers she wore in her bosom.

Having visited the principal places where the Israelites encamped, during their forty years sojournment in the wilderness, they reached the Red Sea, on the shore whereof, Herennianus standing, repeated in a loud and impressive tone of voice, the exulting song of Moses.

Zenobia proceeded forward to Egypt, but did not tarry longer there than requisite to adjust the public concerns of her new realm; for her mind returning with eagerness to the principal object of her journey, on quitting Africa, she requested Theodosius to proceed without delay to Bethlehem and Jerusalem.

They skirted the western shores of the Dead Sea, nor stopped until they reached the fountains of Solomon, and here, by the queen's command, her tents were pitched. The youths drank at the sacred spring, and examined with interest the three pools, each supplying the other in beautiful cascade, and looked around on what was once the gardens and vineyards of the Jewish king; but, of which, the sword of war had swept away every vestige.

The company had dispersed various ways, and Theodosius and Zenobia with her sons alone remained. These fields, remarked the patriarch, were once the fields of Boaz, and herein gleaned the virtuous Ruth, here David fed his flocks, and tuned his harp to the praises of God.

'The Lord is my shepherd, therefore can I lack nothing,' repeated Timolaus— 'He shall feed me in a green pasture, and lead me forth beside the waters of comfort; he shall convert my soul.'— Zenobia looked at Theodosius, and the expression of that look could not be misunderstood.

Having proceeded on for some time in silence, the patriarch stopped, and pointing upward, said, Behold yon summit crowned with groves; there is the city of David, that is Bethlehem.—Bethlehem! exclaimed Zenobia, O hasten hither.—Hold! interrupted the patriarch, thou hast first many interesting places to visit—the Tower of Ebal, where the shepherds fed their flocks at night, when the glory of the Lord shone before them; the house of Simeon, to whom it had been foretold, that he should not see death before he had seen the Lord's Christ, the tomb of Rachel Jacob's wife, and the dwelling of Joseph the husband of Mary.

And yonder then, repeated Zenobia with holy emotion, is Bethlehem Ephrata, expressly mentioned by the prophet Micah; and hither travelled from Nazareth the young and pious virgin, then fourteen years of age, the daughter of Joachim and Anna of the tribe of Judah, a long and wearisome journey for one thus circumstanced, here to give birth to him who was promised to Eve.—Why longer delay visiting Bethlehem, there I purpose tarrying some days, for I shall not return in peace to Palmyra, ere I traverse the town throughout; ere I enter that stable; touch that manger.

Stay, O queen! said Theodosius with deep dejection of look and voice, stay, nor attempt to approach it one step further; no nearer to it must thou come, never must thou ascend the hill of Bethlehem, never reach its summit: Seest thou that summit? Seest thou those groves that crown the eastern part?—On the summit is the temple of Adonis, those groves are the groves of Venus.

Struck with horror and amazement, Zenobia stood.—Thou, continued he, the fair example to thy empire of unsullied chastity, pure as the snows of Armenia among which thou wert nurtured, never must thy maternal feet ascend yon eminence: drop thine eye, close thine ear, turn away thy steps, and breathe a purer air, for yonder is the dwelling of impiety and voluptuousness.

The eye of Zenobia was fire, her cheek scarlet, as she firmly crossing her hands upon her bosom, exclaimed, Judea mine! and Bethlehem worship such! temples, groves, and worshippers, shall consume in one fire!—And who, O woman! returned Theodosius, hath commissioned thee to be the minister of vengeance? Art thou an Elijah to call down fire from heaven? —Execute thy purpose, when at thy call fire doth fall; until then usurp not the prerogative of the Almighty.—Destroy the heathen groves and fabric if thou wilt, but presume not to stretch a persecuting hand over the persons of the worshippers.—Invite to conversion by thy own example, hold forth the blessings of peace and truth, and convince all thy subjects that, in thy mind, beautiful are the feet of them that preach the gospel.

Oh, blind ingratitude! repeated Zenobia, thus to turn science and nature into the embellishment of abominations! The building faultless, the architecture perhaps superb, its myrtle groves seem lovely, yet all to be thus dishonoured And are the holy relics utterly destroye

Not so, replied the patriarch, but they are at present, entirely concealed beneath the foundation of yon impious edifice: the stable is a cave, hewn out of the living rock; the manger a shallow concave in the west side thereof, two feet from the floor; the situation of both, ascertained most accurately.

And is it thus with Jerusalem? asked Zenobia, will disappointment also meet me there? — Thou wouldst have been equally disappointed, answered Theodosius, hadst thou visited it some few years back; for, as thou must have heard, on Mount Moriah, where Abraham offered Isaac, and Solomon reared the temple, Adrian had erected an heathen structure: on the spot where once stood the holy altar, he placed a marble pillar, supporting a statue of himself, and having compleated the new city, dedicated it to Jupiter Capitolinus; over the gates, in derision of the Hebrew, he caused to be placed swine cut in marble, and though Christians are permitted to settle within the walls, the Jew is expelled; nay, it is death for any to look, even from the distant tops of the hills, upon the city of their ancestors; O Jerusalem! Jerusalem! thou that stonedst them that were sent to thee, thou that wouldst not know the things appertaining to thy safety; thou grave of the prophets! thou anathemized of the Lord!—Yet dear is Jerusalem to me, continued Theodosius, O most dear: there, on Calvary, have lived my progenitors; there, at Olivet, lie the remains of my deceased children; there do I hope to end my pilgrimage.

Six miles northward, mounting vine and olive covered hills, they discerned on the summit of the highest, the walls and towns of a city; at the first sight of it, Theodosius rode on alone a few paces before the rest, yet gradually lingering his steps, the queen and his friends at length overtook him.

Approaching Zenobia and the princes, he pointed out to them successively, as they rode beside him from place to place, the dwelling of Zachary, the tomb of Elizabeth, the vale of Hinnom, the wall of Nehemiah, the site of Solomon's idolatry, the potter's field, the field of blood, the sepulchre of the Virgin, and the pillar of Absalom.

Herennianus and Timolaus instantly alighting, took up stones and threw them at the tomb of that ungrateful and rebellious son, then ran and fondly kissed the hand their mother held out to them. By the advice of the patriarch, the queen and a few of her train also dismounted, and followed him up a gentle ascent.— This, said he, still ascending, until arrived at a considerable height, is the Mount of Olives ; the torrent we crossed is the brook Cedron, the last valley through which we passed was that of Jehosaphat, yon garden below is the garden of Gethsemane, and here beneath us behold Jerusalem !

Zenobia gazed with speechless emotion, whilst Herennianus and Timolaus, quitting their mother, went on each side of Theodosius, gliding into his their little hands, and looking up anxiously to his expressive face. Mount Moriah, whereon stood the Jewish temple, continued the patriarch, is as thou seest, wholly excluded from the new city; those hills formerly without the walls are admitted, Calvary being now the centre of Jerusalem. Here on this Mount of Olives are the remains of Bethphage, where the multitude cut down branches of palm and strewed them in the way, when Jesus entered the city triumphantly, shouting ' Hosannah to the son of David!' Timolaus searched and found the prophecy in Zechariah, and read it aloud.

The first act of Jesus, said Theodosius, was that of power and judgment, he cast the money changers from out the temple: the next that of mercy and kindness; he gave sight to the blind, and healed all that were brought to him. He then openly proclaimed to the Jews, that he was the corner stone rejected by the builders, and which should yet become the head of the corner, and that the gospel should be preached first to the Hebrew then to the Gentile. In parables he taught them ever to be prepared for death, by leading a life of holiness, and left no doubt of the immortality of the soul, by asserting that Abraham, Isaac, and Jacob, were then in existence. The whole sum of his doctrine is this, 'Thou shalt love the Lord thy God with all thy heart, and thy neighbour as thyself.' His ministry was confined to Judea, but twelve years after the ascension, the apostles spread his name throughout the known world.

Was the gospel planted in Syria? enquired Zenobia. Theodosius looked at her some time in silence—And this, he at last exclaimed, is the end of learning! if such be the fruits of study, be study laid aside: thou, so well versed in the writings of the profane, thus to be wholly ignorant of sacred truths!—Thine is a censure on my mother, replied Zenobia, that I cannot suffer to pass unanswered: Hast thou found me deficient in the Old Testament, in that religion in which I was reared? is not thine new to me, but lately examined into? was I even compelled to know that such existed?

Thou wert, replied the patriarch; true taste and genius must have prompted thee to enquire into the doctrine of that sect, so renowned as hath been the Christian during the two last centuries; to have discovered what was that wonderous hope which strengthened, and still doth strengthen the disciples of Christ to suffer patiently all the evils inflicted in the last eight persecutions; by what spirit were they inspired to speak new languages, emboldened in proclaiming their faith, and fortified to endure all things, to embrace poverty, to return good for evil, and to live in charity with all mankind. This had been a study worthy thy genius, far more than perusing a second time, much less spending years in dwelling on the beauties of those who wrote how Troy was sacked, Carthage founded, Italy peopled. The siege of Jerusalem is far more interesting than that of Troy, and if made the study of youth, would lead the youthful mind to enquire into the cause of its destruction, and thereby teach it that it is the hand of God that lays the foundation of cities, and the same hand that crumbles them into dust.

Turning to the youths, who listened with eager attention; You have both, he said, doubtless read Pliny with Longinus, what testimony doth he bear of the Christian?—We do not remember, they replied.—Pliny says, that their whole crime is to worship God and their Redeemer, to observe religious rites, to keep their word, and be faithful to each other.

Who preached the gospel in Syria, holy father? asked Zenobia.—St. Jude, one of the twelve apostles, who suffered martyrdom in the East for reproving the rites of the magi. Although seven churches were planted in Asia, and Christianity widely spread in those regions, yet so firmly rooted is paganism, in Syria particularly, that the hand of armed power can alone root it out. This, Zenobia, is an awful period, the world being now divided between various and contradictory opinions: the worshipper of Jupiter, the adorer of the crocodile, him that doth homage to the stone beneath his feet, the Eastern, who bows before the sun and never-dying fire, the Arabian-believer in the God of Ishmael, the Jew-believer in the God of Isaac, and the Christian. If that Revelation spread not early and rapidly through these parts, some wild infatuated enthusiast, taking advantage of the absurdities of all religions but one, and the lack of fervour in that one, may be tempted to raise a new standard of faith, equally inimical to all, but most to the luke-warm Christian. One deeply read in the human heart, the Asiatic character, may be permitted for a time as a scourge to the slow progress of Christian knowledge, to lift a daring hand and say, Be deaf to those, hear me; a sect who may be suffered to enjoy their hour, and O, to all of other faith, how dreadful may prove that hour! it will not last for ever, but do thou, Zenobia, strive to prevent it—be thou the instrument in the hand of heaven to avert the evil.

Is Longinus a Christian? asked Timolaus. Theodosius and Zenobia looked at each other, when the patriarch, as if the request had been already made, said, on my return to Palmyra I will attempt it: of virtuous heathens; and there have been many, he is the first; his feelings are strong, genius ardent, and sensibility acute. Thou must not for a time employ him in worldly affairs, but make secretary any other, and on his conversion or rejection of the gospel, let him resume the office; if converted, he will be a firm prop to thy new faith, if otherwise, God is the judge of hearts.—Dost thou know him personally? asked Zenobia.—I never saw him but once, and never spoke with him; no man will dare hold himself out to the world otherwise than he is, for such hypocrisy would be an insult to God, the searcher of hearts. I judge of Longinus by his writings.

Descending from the Mount of Olives on the southern side, to the summit of which Theodosius promised to bring them ere their final departure, they mounted their horses and camels, and visited Bethany; they entered the house of Simon the Leper, that of Martha and Mary, and the sepulchre of Lazarus, and visited the fountain of the apostles.

Skirting the foot of Mount Olivet, they passed the spot where the traitor Judas died, and continuing their course, entered the garden of Gethsemane. Hither, said Theodosius, (the last passover celebrated by our Lord and his disciples,) he came to prepare for the hour of death: yonder he left them overpowered with sleep, and on the spot where we now stand he knelt in solitude and prayer, from hence he was taken that same night forcibly back to the city; this to the right is the road he trod—it is the road to Jerusalem; we will follow it. He was brought before Caiaphas, who sat in judgment with the priests and elders, and delivered in the morning to Pilate, the Roman governor. 'His blood be upon us and our children!' exclaimed the Jews, and thirty-seven years after, Jerusalem was drowned in their blood and that of their children.

Theodosius paused, and looked upon Zenobia; he saw the emotions to which his speech had given rise, and pointing forward as they rode along, There remains but one more object of interest and curiosity; come and behold it: but as the determination of Judea to place itself under thy protection is not yet universally made known, it is requisite still to conform to the present regulations, to be amenable to the existing government. This city is yet under Roman power; let us not now dispute that power, but conform to its laws. Although no Hebrew may here enter, thou, as a Christian, art privileged; in order therefore to avoid all painful distinction between thy Hebrew and Syrian train, leave the whole yonder in the Vale of Jehosaphat until our return, and enter Jerusalem with me, accompanied only by thy sons.

I looked to find my uncle Elkanah here, remarked Zenobia, as they went towards the city, for he obeyed not my order of recal.—I know not whither Elkanah went on leaving Palmyra, replied Theodosius, but be assured, O queen, he was never suffered to enter Jerusalem.

As they approached the eastern walls, Theodosius stopped to point out the place where St. Stephen was stoned, and then entered the gate bearing that holy martyr's name. It having been thus previously arranged by the patriarch's interest with the Roman inhabitants, and his authority over the Christian, they met not a human being in their almost silent progress from the gate of St. Stephen to the western part of the city. The speech of Theodosius gradually softened into a whisper, and Zenobia and the princes appeared as scarcely venturing to breathe. There, said the patriarch, to our left, is the Pool Bethesda and the site of Pilate's house; here are the stairs that lead to the judgment-seat. Yonder, to our right, once stood the palace of Herod—this is the Dolorous way; we pass the gate of justice: and here is Mount Calvary.

They ascended the rocky hill: on its summit was seen a small projection of the rock a few feet higher than the other part; Theodosius stepping hastily forward, pointed to it with strong tokens of emotion, and Zenobia guessed the spot. In silence she took from her elder son the Greek Testament she had given him in charge, and when her feelings would thus permit her, read aloud from the seizure of Jesus in the garden to his expiring on the cross; and as with awe and veneration she lowered the book, she gazed intently upon the place whereon that cross had stood, and in imagination still beheld hanging thereon, the suffering body of the Saviour of the world.

Reflect, said Theodosius, on the occupation at that moment of the Roman soldiers who crucified him; were they not parting his garments among them, and casting lots for his vesture? Thou, Zenobia, lookest upon David as a prophet? —The most holy, the most favoured, and the most truly inspired, she replied.— Then, continued Theodosius, Read these passages in the Psalms in which the several particulars of the Redeemer's passion are set forth so clearly and distinctly. Now say, Zenobia, thou so perfect in knowledge of all historical events from the earliest times to the present, canst thou recal any other of mankind to whom these passages are applicable?— Thou art skilled in the antient Hebrew, the modern Syriac, the Egyptian, Greek, Persian, and Latin languages; few, if any books in these, it appears, have escaped thy notice: I am not thus skilled. Canst thou enlighten me, and say in whom, except in Jesus Christ, has this prophecy been fulfilled?—But mine, he added, is a Christian Bible; we Christians may since the resurrection have introduced these psalms and other passages into the prophets. Where is the passage in thine own genuine Jewish Bible?

Here, as thou art well assured, replied the queen, taking it from Timolaus. This Bible was given to my mother by hers, who received it from her father Ehi, a scribe and doctor of the law; this copy descends to me through ten generations, and was made ere the last captivity, some centuries before the birth of Christ.

Oh, exclaimed the patriarch, what words can be found to excuse the hardened, the blind. the bigotted Hebrew, who for ages in possession of the prophets, yet spurns the truth that every prophecy is already fulfilled! Now mark the triumphant conclusion of one of those psalms, which so punctually describes the circumstances of our Saviour's passion, and which Christ repeated, as to say, 'Return to your homes, open the scriptures, read that psalm, and believe in me.'

Theodosius ceased, and soon after conducted Zenobia to the holy sepulchre, pointing out in their way thither the natural rent in the rock of Calvary. Here, said he, is the tomb of Joseph of Arimathea; Jesus made his grave with the rich—he here reposed in death, and on the third day rose again triumphantly. As thou hast read, he appeared at sundry times to his disciples for forty days—they saw him, they felt him, they conversed with him; we saw not those things, but blessed are they who seeing not, do yet believe.

Curiosity and zeal thus amply satisfied, Zenobia quitted Jerusalem, and conducted by Theodosius, returned to Mount Olivet, where, on the centre height, she perceived a multitude of people assembled, to whom, on approaching, the patriarch pointing, said, Behold my flock, the Christian brethren of Calvary! On this spot our Saviour, after he was risen from the dead, spake to his disciples for the last time, saying, 'Go ye into the world, and preach the gospel—he that believeth and is baptized, shall be saved.' Whilst Jesus was thus blessing them, a cloud received him out of their sight; and while they, as thou dost, naturally following the direction of my hand, looked stedfastly towards heaven as he went up, behold angels in white apparel there appeared, saying, 'Ye men of Galilee, this same Jesus who is taken up from you, shall so come down from heaven to judge the world.'

Theodosius only ceased speaking, when his Christian flock, headed by their bishop, and accompanied by their families, in number about seven hundred, slowly gathered to the spot where he stood with the queen; in awe and silence they looked at both, when, pointing to Zenobia, Theodosius said, Behold my brethren, a future member of our church, a child of God, and I trust, an inheritor of the kingdom of heaven.

Zenobia knelt, and the congregation also kneeling, their patriarch, standing on a gentle eminence, stretched forth his hands in fervent prayer, which having concluded, he addressed the assembly, saying aloud, Thus is my mission to Palmyra most gloriously fulfilled!

END OF THE NINTH BOOK.

ZENOBIA,

QUEEN OF PALMYRA.

BOOK X.

ARGUMENT.

Zenobia's return to Palmyra—Takes a survey of the suburbs of the city—Her reflections in the valley of the sepulchres—Is met by her father—The views of Elkanah considered—Through his means, Porphyry has accompanied him to Palmyra—Paulus returns from Antioch, and Theodosius is for a time removed—Heathenism revives—Antiochus urges the queen to new conquests—His advice is supported by many, and opposed by Orodes—The Roman province of Bithynia taken by Zabdas—Theodosius returns to Palmyra—The festive hall—The interview of the patriarch with Septimia and the young princes—The death of Septimia.

DID ever nation fall unwarned? Individuals are reminded of the consequences of iniquity, and are not nations also? What then, O Palmyra, was thy warning? Did fearful comets hang (sad funeral lamps!) over thee, as over Jerusalem? Did one bewailing run through thy streets, as in Sion, crying, Woe, woe to Palmyra! Didst thou also hear a voice in thy temple, saying, Let us be gone?—Not one of these awful signs was given thee, beloved city, but like a thief in the night, destruction came upon thee. And yet, O lamentable remains of grandeur unparalelled! you cannot lift up your ruined head, and say, I fell unwarned. On the day that thy sovereigns returned from their southern journey, there was not on earth a city to be compared with thee.

Snows of the north! exclaimed Zenobia, as she caught again the first sight of Lebanon, from your white bosom I may discern the boundaries of my native land. Its queen returns to her dear, her precious hive, laden with luxuriant mental spoils gathered in the mountains of the South.

Nor were these the only fruits of her

expedition: those of her train, entrusted with the commission, had well fulfilled her orders, and above a score of camels were laden with various productions both natural and artificial, destined to adorn, improve, and beautify Palmyrene and its capital; among these were balm from Jericho, sweet canes from Arabia, flowers from Damascus, and a variety of fruit trees from the same luxuriant neighbourhood; at Tyre and Sidon they had collected specimens of every manufacture, and had prevailed on many skilful artificers of those places to accompany them back to their city.

It was evening when Zenobia reached the outskirts of Palmyra. Victorinus, presenting himself before her, awaited in silence the watch-word. *Zenobia,* she softly said, and with his troops he disappeared. The word *Zenobia* was ever the order for a silent and private reception; whereas *the queen* is come back, *the queen* is arrived, was the signal for martial music, unfurled banners, acclamations, entire cessation of business, and the coming forth of the tribes to hail their monarch's return.

Ever on the throne would have rendered to Zenobia a throne irksome, but often to descend a few steps, and sometimes even to mingle with her subjects, was to her the most captivating charm of royalty; yet with a jealous eye she ever watched that throne, and if any unhallowed footstep dared encroach a single step, the way kept clear, like lightning she would rushing mount, and reassume the sceptre.

Arrived at the entrance of the wood of Palmyra, Zenobia alighted, and sending forward her train, slowly followed, attended only by Theodosius, Victoria, and her sons; slow were her steps, for at every step she lingered to examine, to enjoy. She passed a cheerful party near the vale of aloes, seated in the rays of the setting sun, around one who recited with appropriate gestures, a tale of wonder, and as her garments brushed the reciter, glancing downward, she caught the look of astonishment and the smile of incredulity, mixed with that of eager curiosity to hear the conclusion They looked up—a silent salute was' the only return made to her silent wave of the hand.

At some distance were groups of young men exercising, and on the opposite side of the valley companies of maidens employed in spreading flakes of wool upon the grass to catch the pure night dew; various shepherds were driving home their flocks, or watering them at the spring, whilst their wives were engaged among the kine. Passing the ripe vineyard, Zenobia remarked, Do not my mountains literally drop sweet wine, and my land overflow with milk and honey?

They skirted the gardens and a wide plantation of olive, fig, and mulberry-trees, the fruit of which beauteous laughing children were gathering and eating; and drew near an aged and infirm Palmyrenian, who was seated at the door of his tent, canopied by a spreading vine; he held on his knee a cake of bread and a piece of honey-comb, and was enjoying this his evening meal, when Zenobia approached. In haste to rise, his trembling hands eagerly endeavoured to collect the scattered fragments, when the whole fell to the ground. Nor Herennianus nor Timolaus moved a step to relieve his anxiety and distress, which Theodosius observing, advanced before them, and stooping, gathered the fallen food, and restored it to the aged man, on whose white and palsied head Zenobia laid her hand, saying, Peace be unto thee, most honoured father. He looked after her, and never from that hour to the day of his death, did he fail repeating to all who would listen to him, this proud incident, or ever forget the pressure of that hand.

On the borders of the river, the queen remarked several caravans newly arrived from Sura and Alalis, and others preparing to depart in the morning for the West; bales of rich goods were piled in pyramids in the centre of the valley, and covered with thick hides, to preserve them from the night air' The camels, horses, and mules being turned loose to graze far and wide, and browse as choice directed, yet were ever ready to obey the order of recal, for they knew neither goad, nor spur, nor lash; rest was to them refreshment, and exertion welcome exercise.

Zenobia perceived that her orders respecting the exposed aspect of the East had been obeyed, and various plantations of fir, box, larch, and oak sprinkled as directed; some were completed, others only begun, and the scattered tools of the workmen marked out the designed places. She walked to a favourite spot, a gentle eminence, whence issued the springs that supplied the aqueduct, and beheld with pleasure that her wishes there had also been executed; it now bore the appearance of a garden, and on it flourished the black and yellow rose, the purple bind-weed, the small-leafed star of Bethlehem, the richly tinctured wall-flower of Armenia, and the pale, yet lovely Iris.

Following the course of the water, they reached the broadest part of the river, and Zenobia examined what progress had been made in her absence in the great and important undertaking of deepening and widening that river, in order to render it navigable, and thereby open a communication with the Euphrates. The workmen had not yet quitted the spot, and in silence she watched them at their labour; they saw her observing them, and the wearied arm acquired fresh vigour.

On entering the solitary valley of the sepulchres, Zenobia stopped, and leaning on the entablature of that near at hand, (a lofty tomb overshadowed by lime-trees) she looked around with fond emotion. After a long pause, It is observed, she at length said, that early youth is the season of happiness, of enjoyment—is not rather maturity, or even age? In youth, all being new to our senses, we enjoy without discrimination, without consciousness; but on numbering many years, retrospection becomes ours—sorrow gone by fades, and happiness strengthens—every past grief is softened to a charm, and every joy remembered with double transport. I saw this spot now many years since for the first time: it was evening; the sun, as now, was setting; the air was, as at present, perfumed with the sweet odours of the lime-tree; the only sound then was the song of the nightingale, and what sounds now are heard but my voice and the song of that sweet bird? I leaned at that hour on this same tomb, all wonder, doubt, and surprise: bewildered, unconscious who, where, or what I was; when I look back upon that moment ! unconscious then, but now! O what an instant of bliss appears that when for the first time I entered the walls of my own Palmyra.

Victoria listened, and not one word passing to her heart, she could answer Zenobia cheerfully—Theodosius listened, and could make no reply.

The swallows are building in the pinnacles of the temple, remarked Herennianus, when they walked forward; how gaily do they flutter in circles round the city, as if to thank us for their protection!—My mother, said Timolaus, behold how the stock of Tyrian purple fish are encreased in the fountain under Trajan's wall. The birds have built their nests in the battlements of the castle. How beauteous are the western fortifications thus crowned with golden flowers! And see, a young date-tree, perchance self-sown, has sprouted from the summit of the tower of Solomon!

They entered the city, and were met in the gateway by Antiochus and Artabazus, and as would the humblest family in Palmyra, the queen and hers walked through the streets towards the palace. At every door, at every casement and window were seen clusters of joyful faces, seldom was the whole person visible; stooping out and drawing back with smothered whispers of congratulation of 'Zenobia *is* returned,'—and when they had passed, again leaning forward to look after them.

The weary, yet satisfied artificer, returning from daily labour barely moved his head, as he hurried homeward to enjoy the fruits of that labour; the craftsman still at work, scarcely suspended his toil, to remark those that passed; the saunterer alone stopped to gaze; and the invalid, retiring from the evening air, alone bowed as the royal party crossed him.—A word was not spoken, a sound was not breathed, but stolen looks of transport well explained how great their pleasure, that the queen was come back: nor could love or homage be better expressed, than by strict obedience to her known commands.

At the palace she found Orodes, the procurator, and prince of the senate waiting to receive her; when, appointing the next day for a day of audience, she retired with her mother to her private apartments. Victoria hastened to her own palace to enquire, was her husband Claudian yet arrived from Rome. Theodosius repaired to the house of Irenius, and Caleb, by Zenobia's desire, took charge of Omar the Arab:—the charge of a wild camel's colt would have been to Caleb more welcome.

Zabdas, having objected to Omar's admittance into Palmyra, he was lodged that night at a house in the suburbs; but ere the sun arose, and whilst yet the streets were empty, the houses being still shut, and the markets unvisited, Omar was found, by one of the night centinels, walking leisurely through a square in the centre of the city: on being questioned how he had gained entrance, he pointed to a raven perched on the walls, which, as he spake, flew down into the street beside him.

Caleb now appeared seeking Omar,

and having found, he was conducting him back, when, he perceiving the houses and shops gradually open, entered all those near him, successively gliding swiftly in, and as swiftly rushing out, examining all things, and handling their wares and merchandize, wholly regardless of the amazement and confusion his appearance created. Thus pursued he his lawless course through the greatest part of the city, still restless and impatient, appearing in search of a lost treasure, until he arrived before the royal palace; when, giving a sudden scream of joy he rushed past the guard and disappeared through an arch-way.

All within was in a moment uproar and consternation, the voices of women were heard, and Caleb had reached the foot of the staircase leading to the apartments of the females, when he met Omar stealing softly down (a couching leopard with his prey), carrying, in his arms, the half-naked and sleeping Timolaus: the alarm was instantly given without, the guards appeared, and the Arab was compelled to relinquish the child to Caleb, who, ascending to Zenobia's apartments, had him conveyed by her women to his mother.

When, that some hours after, Omar was summoned before the queen, the undaunted Arab, looking alternately at those assembled, fixed on Elkanah as the father of Timolaus, and addressed him—Thou hast three children, and he pointed to the princes.—I have not one; give me that bright-eyed boy for son.—I would, with pleasure, replied the cold unfeeling Elkanah, were he mine to give, but he does not belong to me, he belongs to the queen.

Name any other reward, good Omar, said Zenobia, and thou shalt have it, for in our journey thou wert a kind, indulgent, and faithful guide. When he was in thy power, thou didst not attempt it; why now have endeavoured to deprive me of my little son?—I took an oath on the black stone of Emessa, replied Omar, to bring him back in safety to this city, but I did not swear to let him remain here: ransom him for ten bales of black cloth for tents for my tribe. Give him thirty, said the queen, and besides six change of raiment, let him have from the treasury a talent of silver

The cloth is sufficient, interrupted Elkanah, why should the monies of the public treasury be lavished on this lawless pillager, this camel-feeding Arab, this licensed robber of the desert?—Omar, grinning horrible vengeance, would have darted with strangling hands upon Elkanah, had not the queen stood before and protected him.—Give me the head of that man! roared the incensed Arab. 'I would, with pleasure, dear Omar, were it mine to give, replied Zenobia, but it does not belong to me, it belongs to my uncle.'—His head shall yet be mine, muttered Omar, retreating and touching his scymitar.

Being informed by Caleb, that the bales of cloth, change of raiment, and bags of silver were prepared, and two dromedaries and their leaders to attend him, he approached Zenobia, and gently took from her hand a cornelian seal, which he was putting on his own finger, when she explained that, it being that wherewith she sealed edicts and other papers of state, he readily relinquished it, and she threw over his neck a chain of emeralds. He then drew near the princes: from the waist of Herennianus, he softly took a girdle of silk, and, stooping, unfastened from the ancle of Timolaus a golden ring; having adorned himself with both, the girdle on his arm and the anclet on his wrist, he stood some time looking, alternately and with pleasure, at the queen's gift and his own purloinings from the youths: then casting one fond look on Timolaus and the dire glance of revenge on Elkanah, he sprang to the door, and to the joy and relief of all present disappeared.

The hour of public council, fixed by Zenobia for the ensuing day, was succeeded by that of private audience. Elkanah, thou hadst thine; returned from Tyre, and not from Jerusalem, thou demandedst of the queen, an early and a secret interview, and it was granted. Orodes, Antiochus, Longinus, Statirus, and Timagenes; all, all had theirs.—O what several, what clashing, and opposite interests do these names imply?

On Elkanah's arrival at Tyre, the news followed him, of the coming of Theodosius to Palmyra, and of the ascendancy that the patriarch had gained over both Zenobia and Septimia. Could then, Elkanah proceed to Judea? No; to avert the threatened destruction of his hopes, he straitway returned to Syria; not alone, alas! but accompanied by the renowned Porphyry, who urged to compliance, by the repeated messages of Longinus, and the pressing invitation of Zenobia at length consented, under the conduct of Elkanah, to visit Palmyra.

Ere, however, they could arrive, Zenobia and Theodosius had departed for Judea.

For Judea! repeated Elkanah, as he entered his study, and closed the door, and seated himself at his table.—True, Elkanah did not accompany the queen and patriarch in their journey, but what proceedings of theirs could be concealed from this rich and powerful Hebrew, who numbered among Zenobia's Jewish followers, many, by interest devoted to him heart and soul?—The meditations of Elkanah were disturbed by Hyrcanius, the priest of Apollo; the great admirer of Porphyry and his writings.—Would that we were able to prevail on this illustrious platonist, to prepare for the queen's return, a brilliant effusion of genius.—To this observation of Hyrcanius, Elkanah made no reply, but the same day, at his instigation, Porphyry resumed the pen, and shortly after, produced a wondrous treatise.—Elkanah, having perused it, pronounced it admirable.—Excellent, repeated Hyrcanius.—Unanswerable, said Orodes, Antiochus, and Caleb. —Be the Christian the judge of the nature of that treatise commended by the Hebrew, admired by the Pagan.

Art thou satisfied, Elkanah?—Not wholly so, Paulus of Sarmosata must also arrive, and Theodosius at his return be removed, then will the subtle Israelite wrap himself in the thick folds of security.

Not many days after this general day of audience, and Paulus accused of heresy, was, at the instigation of Aurelian, a second time deposed by the synod of Antioch: when, like a raging flame, he burst into Palmyra, calling down the vengeance of Zenobia on the Roman, who had thus presumed to interfere in the government of a Syrian province; not many days, and disturbances brake out among the Christians of Apamea; though none knew the cause, when Theodosius was sent thither by the queen, to restore peace and good order.

Thus was Porphyry, the bitterest enemy of the church, received into the devoted city; thus was Paulus, the unbelieving Christian re-admitted; and thus, was Theodosius the friend of God and man for a time excluded; and in that time, that short space—O, slowly doth the blessed grain increase, but rapid is the growth of tares!—O, Elkanah! at the fall of Palmyra, canst thou hope to escape the crash of ruins?—Will not the very beam of the timber bear witness of thy craft, and the stones of the wall cry out against thee?

The consequences of these changes were speedily perceived, declining heathenism revived, and Christianity a beauteous rising lily, was nipped in its growth; groves and high places encreased, and not a town or village that did not boast its idol, and attendant abominations.

Why not? enquired Antiochus; why not, when in Egypt, have embarked for Italy? one sight, though distant, of imperial Rome had inspired the breasts of these youths with imperial hopes, my grandsons might have said—' Europe is a goodly field, would it were added to my garden.'—Naboth's vineyard—Ahab's fate, my father, replied Zenobia; nature herself has limited us Asiatics to Asia. —Yet the Europeans, answered Antiochus, scorn to limit themselves to Europe, or why does Roman power, though now rapidly on its decline, even stretch east of the Euphrates? thy sons may yet add the Roman to their Syrian purple.

The gods forbid, exclaimed Orodes, that Palmyra should ever again become subject to Rome!—Why thus pervert my meaning, retorted Antiochus, which thou must suppose is to subject Rome to Palmyra?—It cannot be, said Orodes; the more extended, the weaker the empire: Palmyra, like Greece, may stand against the armed world, whereas the almost boundless Roman power may yet be undermined by a single savage tribe. Thou, Antiochus, lookst solely to family aggrandizement, unmindful of the real welfare of thy native land, for provided thy posterity enjoy unlimited sovereignty in any part of the globe, Palmyra may sink overwhelmed in its own sands; but I love Palmyra, and Palmyra chiefly, therefore to secure her safety advise no fresh conquests.

Queen Zenobia, said Zabdas, sieze on Bithynia, and thus, by opening a passage into Europe through Byzantium, Europe may yet be thine.—And Europe hers, exclaimed Orodes, passionately, yet with grief and tenderness; and what becomes of Palmyra? a desert watering trough for camels, a deserted harbour for plundering Arabs, caves and holes for bears and serpents—may I die ere that day—one loose stone in yonder street, one blade of grass growing on this wall is dearer to me than the world, and my voice shall not cease night and day to cry—No new conquest! no fresh subjugations!

And what is the advice of my uncle? asked Zenobia.—To take Bithynia, replied Elkanah, but not attempt to retain it; nay, the attempt will be vain. When reclaimed by Aurelian, yield it as the ransom of the descendants of those of our nation, taken prisoners to Rome at the sacking of Jerusalem.

But hast thou reflected, asked Zenobia, that Bithynia is not as Egypt and other provinces, conquests of Rome, but a rightful possession? Nicomedes, the king, at his death, bequeathed it to that nation, whose it has been more than three centuries—Then touch it not, exclaimed Longinus; touch it not, or heaven will punish the unlawful seizure! —Had heaven punished Rome its many unlawful seizures, remarked Porphyry, what had Rome been now? Listen, queen, to the voice of Antiochus, Elkanah, and others, who prove to thee that Bithynia, in Asia, being the last link of the chain of Asiatic provinces, ceased to belong to Rome when Syria, in the name of the East, asserted and obtained independence, in the reign of Valerian. Thus would thy empire form a beauteous Asiatic bow, Egypt and Bithynia the extremities, and the arrow of war drawn by our divine Amazonian queen to the centre, Palmyra, repel every enemy.—But, remarked Zenobia, should thy archer have but one arrow, and that one overshoot its mark?—No fear, added Statirus, gaily, while Persia and Parthia are quivers inexhaustible.

O miserable statesmen are you all!—Thus in a familiar domestic meeting, in Zenobia's apartment, was kindled the spark of danger, and that spark was never quenched! what was at first only slightly spoken of, was gradually listened to and adopted; daily councils were called, and secret preparations made, for not by violence but subtlely was the purpose to be accomplished. By the counsel of Longinus, who refrained from discussion when he found himself opposed by the queen, the senate, and the people, the coveted province was not to be taken by force of arms, but secretly invited to place itself under Zenobia's protection.

Firmius, a rich merchant of Sidon, who was present at the last deliberation, being lately returned from Bithynia, confirmed their hopes, by making known the estimation in which the name and power of Zenobia was there held. My gold shall do it, said the gigantic Firmius, and the smile of the queen shall repay me. I heard lately from Italy, that the Gauls had rebelled, and that the Goths not being wholly subjugated, Aurelian is at this hour preparing to attack and crush them ; this then is your hour, in his absence it may be done. The province you mark for yours is a stepping stone from Chalcedon in Asia, to Byzantium in Europe, and by my hand it shall be overlaid with gold, worthy the tread of a Zenobia.

Seize it then, O queen, said Paulus ; speedily possess thyself of this rich prize, thou! sovereign of millions who, wouldst thou but display thy power, mightst in thy own person revive, nay exceed the splendour of Darius, Xerxes, and Ahasuerus.—Thou, a being of matchless virtue, added Porphyry, an enthroned Diana, more divine than mortal, who has only to appear, and universal worship is paid thee.

O Alexander, and thou Herod, when ye suffered yourselves to be called gods! ——but Zenobia! what excuse, what motive to palliate her crime? Could she but have known that this was *her* hour of temptation!—all have that hour — temptations adapted to the peculiar circumstances of each. Zenobia could not be tempted by ambition, for she was already great; nor with riches, for gold was in Palmyra of no account; neither with worldly pleasures in any shape—in what shape then could Zenobia be tempted, but in the false insinuating one of adulation? not flattered for beauty, power, or wealth, but virtue!——Deep are thy snares, O enemy of man! this is thy hour, and alas, thou art triumphant: her angel, her guardian Theodosius is absent, and when he does return he comes too late.—Bithynia's taken, and in those two words is comprised the fate of Palmyra.

Few and faithful are those of the Christian college, who, with their pastor Irenius, attentive to their respective duties as citizens, conforming to the laws of the state, and living in harmony among each other, scarcely know the transactions of that state; on the return of Theodosius therefore, ignorant of the many changes that had taken place in his absence, they could not prepare him for those changes and having arranged with him affairs of a private nature, saw him cheerfully depart for the palace.

Hitherto, by Zenobia's orders, the patriarch had been admitted to every apartment, a few excepted, and at all hours, with the same freedom as Antiochus himself; he went forward therefore towards the queen's private study, expecting no impediment, when he was stopped at the foot of the great staircase by a centinel, who demanded who and what he was. Theodosius looked up, and that look was sufficient passport, the man drew back respectfully, and the patriarch ascended.

On the first landing, he was again challenged, and here, though conscious that his person was well known, he was forced to give his name: he went through a line of soldiers and servants, and on reaching the door of the lesser hall, was accosted by a page with extended hand, who said, If thou hast a prayer to make the queen, I will see it delivered to her; then looking up, he confessed his error, made profound obeisance, and let him pass. The hall was empty—he traversed it, and meeting a child, asked, where was the queen?—On the throne, replied the boy; and Theodosius proceeded hastily to the great hall of audience.

He entered—Zenobia was indeed enthroned, and though a multitude was present, of all ranks and ages, Theodosius alone was standing—the whole were prostrate; some lying prone on the marble flooring, and others, their heads in their hands, kneeling on the lower steps of the throne—the usual salutations and forms of homage seemed now to be converted to a system of adoration—not now that outward reverence to royalty, which reason never yet refused to pay, but an impious idolatrous form, which struck Theodosius with speechless astonishment.

The queen thus seated, the patriarch thus standing, the people thus prostrate, Zenobia and Theodosius appeared as if alone, they twain seemed in solitude: he looked at her with a look of surprise and indignation, and in that she read—What outward form of worship then is reserved for God? But when, the next moment, he saw that brilliant eye sink beneath his, that cheek pale with pride and indifference, redden with a sudden feeling of humility, when he beheld the crowned head droop, and the sceptre lower; a drop of balm came over his grieved heart, and he said, as he turned hastily to quit the spot, All is not over; all is not yet lost; what, O what can have produced this! Would that I had not quitted her; never will I again: yet, is this the dependence on her firmness, her rectitude! is this the strength of mind, I weakly thought Zenobia, of all women, possessed.—It was by the will of the Almighty I left her, and she has not been able to withstand the hour of temptation.

On his return to the college he was met by Caleb, and of him the patriarch enquired what had occurred in his short absence.—Only three unimportant events, replied Caleb—The arrival of an aged Tyrian, who threatens soon to rival his more youthful master Longinus, in the favour of the queen, the re-instatement of Paulus in his bishopric at Antioch, and the taking of Bithynia by Zabdas.— Thus, in a few words, was explained to Theodosius, the full extent of every threatened evil; he saw at once the crush of every Christian hope; and, unless timely prevented, by concession to Aurelian, the downfal of the empire.

Should she forsake the cross; should she persecute her new faith! mused Theodosius; whilst still wrapped in thought, an officer appeared, sent by the queen, to desire the attendance of the patriarch at the palace by the next watch.—No, he repeated, all is not yet lost: I shall be yet able to regain my stray one to the paths of justice and safety; and in saving her, I save the kingdom.

The hour came, and Theodosius hastened to pour into her private ear, salutary counsel; what, O what, will be the result! thought the patriarch as he passed forward, and how will she receive it?—Like a rising plant or unfledged bird is this Zenobia, and I an experienced one, with wonder and hope, anxious to know what will be the colours, the note, the plumage!

Again he would have instantly passed

to her study, when he was intercepted by Victorinus, who, being stationed there to receive him, with respectful salutation conducted him to another chamber, which, on entering, he found to be the chamber of festivity.

Ere he crossed the threshold, he surveyed the scene before him, and saw therein nothing to censure. The galleries were filled with minstrels and musicians, one female voice, at the moment he entered, filled the space with harmony, and other women, within a railed platform allotted for the purpose, were dancing; and what Zenobia sanctioned by her presence, was not unbecoming the presence even of a Theodosius; her pleasures were as pure as herself. Yet he would have retreated when beckoned forward by the queen.

Within a few paces of her footstool, he stopped to recognize the group before him: some reclined on couches near her, were conversing with one another, and Victoria and other women sat at her feet, discoursing on the approaching banquet, in honour of the taking of Bithynia. Zenobia was speaking alternately to them and Paulus, who stood behind her with a stranger, whom, on a nearer approach, Theodosius beholding, started as he had seen a spectre—he recognized Porphyry of Tyre! Elkanah was also there, in deliberation with Hyrcanius the high priest of Apollo, and thus surrounded, Zenobia appeared to the patriarch an angel of light encircled by demons.

Zenobia strove to address Theodosius, but faultering with shame and emotion, she could only slightly look a welcome, which those surrounding her, mistaking for cool displeasure, received him with the stare of impertinence and the leer of malignity, whilst some to please their queen as they imagined, treated him with total and pointed neglect. Longinus, alone arose and advancing, kindly pointed to a couch, which Theodosius courteously declining, with melancholy dignity quitted the presence: for a few minutes he lingered among the cheerful throng, and then left the room.

His wandering steps brought him to other apartments, which he entered, in hopes of finding Antiochus whom he had not perceived in the festive chamber; the patriarch again at this threshold, stopped to contemplate a far different sight.—Septimia and a few of her women were seated at a table reading, and at the further end of the room, at their separate tables, with their lamps and books, he beheld Herennianus and Timolaus.

On perceiving Theodosius, they started forward and threw themselves in his arms, then returned in silence to their studies: by Septimia the patriarch was received with equal joy and friendship, for they had not met since his departure with Zenobia on her southern journey, and how great her desire that they should meet ere long!

We shall disturb these young students? remarked Theodosius.—No; replied Septimia, Vaballathus is already gone to rest, and these will soon retire. Thou dost not join the festivities within? he again demanded.—My age and the youth of these boys alike exclude us, she answered; retirement best becomes me, and diligence in virtuous pursuits is their present duty.

And what art thou reading? enquired the patriarch.—The last chapter of the Books of Moses; I have read with Irenius the writings of those recommended by thee, and have, when alone, gone wholly through our scriptures, from Genesis to the Apocalypse. Has not Irenius then informed thee? Art thou as yet ignorant that I am numbered of thy flock? In heart, soul, and belief, I long have been a Christian; I am baptized, confirmed, and received into the communion of saints.

This was indeed most welcome intelligence to Theodosius, and he expressed his pleasure. Could I fail being converted, she said, when, after thy departure for Judea, deprived of my daughter and elder grandsons, I devoted myself to the study of the scriptures, and the writings of the first fathers of the church? I am only astonished that I was not a Christian earlier, and now marvel that the whole world is not such?—And it will, replied Theodosius, but reflect that the grain is now only newly sown; this gathered ten-fold, will again be sown; the multiplied produce will be scattered far and wide; and the day at last come, when the whole globe shall be of one faith: and that faith Christian.

And hast thou attended the church service?—I have; and still daily attend it; not one of its ordinances have I hitherto neglected; but now depressed by bodily weakness, our kind pastor charitably hither comes, sometimes alone, but more frequently with a few of our faith, with whom I discourse and communicate.—And the queen? asked Theodosius—Septimia shook her head.—That aged man, Porphyry of Tyre, is very learned, she replied at length, well skilled in many sciences, and Zenobia encourages him, delighting in his society, but would that she had taken more delight in that of Irenius!

Thou a Christian, mused the patriarch, looking at the young princes, thy husband a pagan, their uncle Elkanah a Jew, and their mother wavering in her faith—what will be the religion of these youths, the future kings of the East?— Septimia was silent, the boys heard the words, and both, at the same instant, advanced and stood before him.—Herennianus, with all the impressive majesty of an infant Jupiter, stretching forth his hand, delivered the whole of the Apostle's Creed; when Timolaus, the gentle lovely Timolaus, kneeling, leaned one arm on the knee of Theodosius and looking in his face, repeated earnestly with lisping voice, the Lord's Prayer, and when he had concluded it, they both again threw themselves on the bosom of Theodosius, saying, This dear father, this is our faith until death.

The youths quitted the apartment, and whilst Septimia gazed fondly after them, Theodosius rising, walked to and fro: when in the dark shade of the room he stopped, and looked at Septimia·— This, then is thy work; be thou blessed, O Septimia, blessed on earth, and thrice blessed hereafter! and thou, Oh Lord, hear the prayer I make thee in her behalf. May her death be as peaceful as her life has been blameless; holy have been her days; holy be her last hour; and O, therein grant her own wishes!

Thus hast thou anticipated the request I designed to make thee, replied Septimia faintly, and is it presumption to say, that never before felt I so well prepared for death, nay, eager to quit this life? all around me is so blissful, so peaceful, so happy, that my soul will smile itself away! doth it not seem a contradiction that I would rather quit the world, beholding those most loved, enjoying felicity, than selfishly escape myself, leaving them to evils and distress.

Theodosius fixed his eyes upon her, and approaching, placed himself at her side. After a short pause, Ere I go, he said, let me advise thee to be ever thus prepared, for the hour of summons may not be distant; thou hast fully accomplished all thy duties here on earth, and must now look for thy reward. Thy conduct during Zenobia's infancy was praise-worthy, thy child had otherwise been heathen, or been sacrificed at the shrine of an idol: thou fleddest not thy husband secretly, but asked and obtained his consent to leave him; and his esteem for thee since thy return, shews how true his confidence in thy virtue. And now farewel, Septimia—farewel: the blessing of God be on thee and thy posterity; be thy days blessed, and when that hour of summons does come, enter the door of salvation opened to thee by the merits of him thy heart acknowledges, the merits and passion of thy Redeemer.

Most solemn, most awful was his look, his voice, his action, when he spake these words, and when he blessed her, as she half-bowing before him, took his revered, his apostolic hand, and raised it to her lips. He quitted her, and when he had reached the door, turned once again to take a lingering, a final look.

It was midnight, when Septimia awaking from a short disturbed slumber, which had been anxiously watched by her women and the queen's physician, sent hither by Theodosius, said, Where is my daughter? Seek her, I pray you. The physician looked and examined, and long was thoughtful; then to the women, You need not disturb the queen, he said; the festivities are now at their height, and she must not be disturbed: all is safe—watch ye, and expect to see me again at sun-rise. The man of science having thus given his directions, left the room, and repaired to his own magnificent apartments adjoining those of the young princes, and in a few minutes was sunk in sleep.

Where is Zenobia? again enquired Septimia. Have ye sought her?

None dare, replied Terentia; none may intrude upon the amusements of the queen, until she gives the signal for them to cease: we cannot go.—I pray you, call my daughter, repeated Septimia, and looked beseechingly from face to face, but no one moved; the deep sigh of despair came from her heart as she reflected on her own helplessness, unable to call other assistance, and she again laid down her head upon her pillow.

Who dared intrude upon the pleasures of the queen! Theodosius dared: from the chamber of Septimia, he returned to that of festivity, and addressing Zenobia, said, Go to thy mother. The severity of the look and tone of voice struck her with dismay, and instantly rising, she quitted the hall.

Art thou ill, my mother? exclaimed Zenobia rushing gently to the bed whereon reposed Septimia. Septimia hastily opened her eyes—her cheek was flushed, and she smiled on those around her, as if to say, Did I not know she would come?— I am not ill, my child; nay, never did I feel so free from pain: a pleasing languor never felt before spreads through my frame, and yet—if thou wouldst but indulge me, Zenobia—I am now one of the aged and infirm; such have often marvellously strange wishes, but if thou wouldst—for this night only place thyself beside me; I will not ask thee another night; and let me sleep again, and sleep in thy arms——

In an instant the diadem, jewels, ornaments, and royal robes glided from the person of Zenobia to the floor, and left her clad in white and simple drapery; she placed herself conveniently for the purpose, and received on her bosom the wasted form of her mother, which she half-encircled by her arms Sabina having related the visit and words of the physician, silence followed, and Zenobia conversed with her attendants only in looks. Yes, said she at length, my mother sleeps; how pure, how calm her delicate features! and her breath warm and fragrant, steals over my cheek, conveying delight! Trim well the lamps, for I will not stir hence until morning. Let no one alarm my father, for this faintness will pass away.

Zenobia watched, until she perceived a gentle shivering run through the limbs of her mother, and felt the deep sigh that followed, with a trembling convulsion of the hand which she held in hers—all again was motionless; slowly lifting the veil thrown over both, she stooped to look upon her face—Her face is pale, whispered Zenobia, and I no longer feel her breath upon my cheek! Her head weighs heavily on my bosom, so heavily I can no longer support it, but must change my posture. Bring hither the lamp, yet cautiously, lest the light disturb her.

The light was brought; again Zenobia raised the veil, softly, tenderly, but at the same moment with frenzied violence she tore it wholly off. Hold! oh, hold! said Terentia, astonished; how ungentle! thou wilt wake thy mother.—Wake her! shrieked Zenobia, wake her! Oh, God! can she be awakened? Look here! Say, it is possible to wake her, and heaven shall hear my cries.

Hath the gentle soul of Septimia yet quitted the bed of death? doth it behold what passes? Look, O blessed spirit, see how thou wert beloved; look upon thy agonized child, clasping thy pale corpse to her bosom; look upon thy husband, drawn hither by her piercing shrieks, standing mute with grief and despair; behold thy beauteous grand-children bursting into tears, refusing comfort—Oh, speak to them, speak to all, and say, Waste not your tears on that; I am here, a being conscious of everlasting bliss. Art thou not seen, O holy spirit? art thou not heard?—Leave then, O leave human nature to indulge the feelings of nature, and do thou wing thy way to heaven and immortality.

END OF THE TENTH BOOK.

ZENOBIA,

QUEEN OF PALMYRA.

BOOK XI.

ARGUMENT.

Longinus reading to the queen his life of Odenathus, and eulogiums on Septimia—Theodosius appears—Reproves and threatens Zenobia — His remonstrances at length produce penitence—She promises the next day to acknowledge her abjuration of Judaism—Breaks her engagement made with the patriarch, in consequence of which he proposes for the Christians to leave Palmyra—The queen refuses her sanction—A meeting of the senate, at which Theodosius warns the Palmyrenians of the consequences of taking Bithynia—Morning—Public rejoicings in honour of Zenobia's new acquisitions—Olympic games—The conquering generals enter Palmyra in triumph—Evening—The royal banquet, at which Zenobia is proclaimed by her subjects Empress of Rome, and her children assume the purple—Orodes incurs the displeasure of the queen, and leaves the hall—Claudian arrives from Rome—His intelligence produces universal dread and consternation.

The days of mourning for Septimia over, and her honoured remains interred in the sepulchre at New Zaantha, Theodosius lost not an hour before he demanded an audience of the queen. Her heart is now made soft by sorrow, said the patriarch; this is the hour of grace, and it must be improved. He found Longinus with her, and this sight inspired him with hope, for he knew how preferable the society of a virtuous heathen to that of an irascible Hebrew, an apostate Christian, or a confirmed Pagan, and such were Elkanah, Paulus, and Porphyry.

Far surpassing thy other works! said Zenobia.—My subject was excellent, said Longinus, fixing his eyes on the ground, as he retired at the entrance of the patriarch.—A well merited eulogium on my mother, said Zenobia, holding the paper to Theodosius, preceded by the life of Odenathus; both shall be read by ages to come.—Neither may ever reach posterity, replied Theodosius; the name of Longinus may, nay, must, but these, thy pride, thy boast, never.

Am I then forsaken? enquired Zenobia, in the voice of penitence.—When are they who keep their faith forsaken? demanded Theodosius. Shall I lead thee back?—And shall I be received? she asked.—Make the attempt: be thy first step to amendment the banishing the pernicious few with whom, in my absence, thou hast been guided, and let me thus lead thee back to the path of peace and good hope.

Zenobia offended that her judgment in the choice of counsellors was thus questioned, replied, Instead of appearing before me to rail against my friends, I expected condolements on my mother, whose loss thou dost not appear to lament, though, when living, thou seemedst to reverence and honour her —Reverence and honour her! replied Theodosius. O how has the timid, unlearned, meek, and simple, surpassed the learned and illustrious! But she rests in peace, secure from coming evil. Has affliction wrought no salutary change, or is thy heart become obdurate through that pressure, as

I read in that imperious frown? And more gloomy, more imperious grew the look of Zenobia, as she waved her hand for him to quit the room. Queen, added he, I will not leave thee.

Thou shalt, she replied, for since thy arrival, like a bird of darkness, thou hast never ceased to flap thy ill-boding wing over Palmyra. My soul overwhelmed with sorrow for my loss, and thou intrude upon my ear with unlikely omens of approaching evils!—I repeat, returned Theodosius, glad is my soul that Septimia is no more, rejoiced I am that she is gone to bliss eternal, ere the days of sorrow come upon this capital of Syria—ere its horses and chariots are cut off, its strong holds are thrown down, its witchcrafts and soothsayers destroyed, its groves of abomination plucked up, and images consumed.

Perceiving that wilfulness and anger had given place to awe and contrition, he added, with parental tenderness, Discard thy advisers; send for them at the instant, that in their presence and thine, I may repeat, discard those serpents, the cause of this sudden change throughout the land, whose impieties, authorized by the Pagan inhabitants of its capital, Palmyra, have risen to a fearful height; neither be guided by their advice in matters of state, for if thy new seizure be not speedily restored to Aurelian, thy fall is inevitable.

Hold! interrupted Zenobia; now thou goest beyond thy duty: confine thyself to religious instructions, and invade not the province of the senator.—And canst thou, Zenobia, he demanded, separate the interests of religion and sound policy, those two arms of the nation? Cut off one, will not the other suffer, nay, endanger the whole body? Restore Bithynia, regain the alliance of Rome, or thy crown passes away.

Govern thou thy church, repeated Zenobia, rising indignantly, and leave that of my realm to me. Let priests keep to spiritual matters, nor presume to interfere with those of state and policy. Theodosius looked at her with undaunted majesty, and then with fervour, repeated, Set up the standard, for the tempest is at hand. Beware! beware! revoke ill counsels ere it be too late.

Oh, cease, replied Zenobia, nor thus depress me into superstition and despair. Religious and civil government truly can have but one interest; yet what wouldst thou have me do? what more than I have already done?—Simply answer me, said Theodosius, this simple question—what art thou? A Pagan, a Jew, or a Christian?—A Christian, she replied.—And is it known to thy subjects? hath it been proclaimed thus to the empire?—No, nor ever shall.—Then thou dost expect to worship God in secret, and deny him to the face of the world?—Reflect, she said, that the established religion of my empire is Pagan.—Did I ever doubt it? Should I otherwise have hither come to preach the gospel?

Thy arguments and zeal are here

misplaced, she answered, for I repeat, that polytheism is too firmly established in Syria ever to be abolished.—This was not thy opinion when in Judea; and who bath since told thee thus? Through shame thou art silent; then hear from me the names of Porphyry and Paulus. O lamentable change in four short months! This the Zenobia whom I beheld in humble adoration at the foot of Calvary! Once more believe me, it is not yet too late; thou hast it still in thy power to place thy realm and self under the best protection: I charge thee, make, ere sun-set, a public acknowledgment of thy faith.

And thus lose the right of sovereignty over a Pagan state, whose population against Christianity is one to a thousand? To avow myself a Christian would be, in the opinion of Paulus, Porphyry, and others, at once to relinquish the crown—Then to Porphyry and Paulus I resign thee; thou advocate for heathenism, to heathen power I give thee for ever up. He would have quitted her, when she caught his robe.

If, added he, gently turning back, thou dost still persist in refusing publicly to own thy having embraced that faith of the truth of which thy judgment is so fully convinced, thou art no Christian, and if no Christian, where is thy refuge in the hour of need? If thou preferest a crown to the love of God, be it so; I, like my divine Master, can only say, How hardly shall they of worldly minds enter into the kingdom of God! But say, Zenobia, from whom dost thou derive this sovereignty? Cannot he who gave it, secure it to thee? It may not be in his wisdom or will to do so, but the alternative can be no excuse for apostacy.— Apostacy! repeated Zenobia. — Yes, dreadful is the word, but to thy case most applicable. The gospel was laid before thee—thou becamest a willing convert, yet ashamed to own thy conversion, will, ere long, relapse into Judaism, if not turn to the worship of the gods of Syria.

And even so, replied the queen, why should Palmyra, why should a nation be punished for my individual transgression?—In temporal dispensations, he replied, there must be a close connection between the interests of many whose circumstances in the last result shall differ widely. I repeat, thy example and that of the worthy Odenathus gained hundreds of Jewish proselytes, and yet to hesitate at gaining converts to the cross! Thou sayest the Christian population is as one to a thousand, but what are thousands against the single voice of truth?

Yet why these precautions? interrupted Zenobia, hastily; I am threatened by no war, no enemy.—No, truly art thou not: the winds of heaven are at this hour most peaceful, the surface of the sandy ocean surrounding thee most calm; but will the winds, the sands be ever thus at rest!

Then, she replied, if doomed to be destroyed, nor power human or divine can avert my destruction.—And is this one of the many doctrines lately imbibed, 'returned Theodosius, from thy Tyrian friend? The prophet and the evangelist shall refute thee:—Nineveh, though threatened, was spared, and to the penitent criminal on the cross was spoken, 'This day shalt thou be with me in Paradise.'

Speak, said Zenobia; only command; and I obey; what wouldst thou of me?'—To morrow, said he, assemble the senate, proclaim thyself a Christian, enter in the face of day, in the face of all thy people, the church of Christ, be baptized, join with us in prayer, and abide the event.—I will, so help me, heaven.

Oh, most awful words—most awful day, the day ensuing! Nor senate was assembled, nor Christian church entered by the queen, she received not the sacrament that awaited her, and yet dared abide the event of this sinful neglect of the holy engagement she had entered into with the patriarch. Zenobia spent the whole of that day, destined to the church and Theodosius, entangled in controversy with the impious Tyrian, and the Bishop of Antioch, both urged on by Elkanah, who had no fears as to her turning Pagan, but the greatest of her proclaiming herself a disciple of Christ, whose in secret he knew she was already become. All hope in Zenobia over, the patriarch, towards the evening of that day, held secret consultation with Irenius and his brethren.

Having arranged all things concerning their future welfare, and drawn up an edict the better to secure that welfare, he went with it to the palace in order to obtain the signature of the queen, whom he found in the senate-house, surrounded by the whole of her new favourites: they were seated, before whom standing, like St. Paul at Felix' tribunal, he told his intentions, and asked the royal permission to put them into instant execution.

Zenobia was amazed. The Christians to remove from Palmyra? And whither wouldst thou have them go?—To any spot upon the globe, replied the patriarch, rather than longer abide in this city.—I have left a blank; do thou speak the destined place, and I will insert it.—Apamea, Emessa, Orthosia, Laodicea, they wish not to leave thy jurisdiction; but it is my advice that they leave Palmyra.

The frozen air of Scythia, said the sarcastic Porphyry, is very conducive to the exertion of every christian virtue.—I regard not where they settle, Paulus exclaimed, provided they come not within sight of Antioch.—A colony of Christians would be very serviceable beyond the Ganges, remarked Elkanah; while Longinus turning to Zenobia, spake with fire, If thou sufferest the Christians to depart, Palmyra loses its best citizens.—

True, said Theodosius; wherefore I would have these virtuous citizens removed ere the hour of destruction come; it is for their sakes, not for the sake of Palmyra, I would place them without delay in peace and security.

Again he offered the roll for her signature, but in vain; she decidedly rejected his prayer, and ordered Orodes to watch that not a christian left the city, —Thou excepted, said Porphyry to Theodosius.—Queen, said the patriarch, taking possession of the elevated seat to which she pointed, thy empire of late extended from the banks of the Euphrates to the shores of the Propontus, from Armenia to Ethiopia, yet thou hast ventured to add to that extent of dominion by rapine and injustice. Woe to him that increaseth that which is not his! Shall they not rise up suddenly that shall vex thee? Thou didst gather unto thee many nations, and heap unto thee all people; yet, still unsatisfied, hast seized upon a province belonging to another master, regardless of the voice which was heard to say, 'The hand that touches Bithynia shall be stricken off!' thus spake Aurelian.

And who and what is Aurelian? demanded Zenobia imperiously.—A soldier, replied Theodosius, rough, untamed, and inflexible, yet prudent and cautious; not the lion, but the crouching tiger, he gives no notice of his approach, but springs on his victim ere it can look around; of majestic countenance, manly grace, athletic figure, hitherto invincible, and until of late the friend of the Christian: he is head of the Roman empire, and god of the Roman armies: such is Aurelian; and now say, Zenobia, what art thou?

Even so, she replied, we are at peace, and Aurelian is my friend.—Then hast thou basely robbed a friend, and in time of peace; without provocation, nay when the Roman sought not to revenge and take back thy other numerous conquests made under his predecessor Claudius. Human laws punish private crimes; God takes on himself to punish those of nations. O Zenobia, imitate the moderation of Adrian, who in time resigned all new conquests! imitate that of thy own revered Odenathus, who was ever heard to declare, that the safety of his empire depended on its strict alliance with Rome.

Empire and *queen!* interrupted Paulus; why should not our sovereign take the more exalted title of *Empress?* and why not our youthful princes here assume the *purple*, independent of the will of Rome?— Thou worst of evil counsellors! exclaimed Theodosius, rising; is it enmity or friendship to Palmyra that prompts this advice? None present have perhaps seen Aurelian, and if they have, but few know him personally; I have, I do: and I tell thee, queen, he begins to look with the eye of jealousy on thy increase of power; the title of Empress, the assumption of the purple without (as in the case of Odenathus) his concurrence, will be the signal of war; defend thy state, thy cities, thy capital, thy freedom, even with life defend them, but prefer moderation and friendship to aggrandizement and rapacious supremacy.

Thou art a friend of Aurelian, said Zenobia, sullenly; but when she looked upon him, added, with meekness, Oh pardon me, most honoured father, my heart is one tumult of anxieties.

If a friend of Aurelian, replied he calmly, what do I in Palmyra? thy nature, queen, is no longer the same; the despotic sovereign of millions, not satisfied with due homage, thou now exactest abject and unhallowed prostration; yet, although in power and magnificence thou far exceedest the most glorious of the Persian monarchs, will never bow the knee in adoration at thy throne, or sooth thee with the false smile of flattery: greater than any Roman emperor art thou, this therefore is the hour selected by me to speak truth to thy ear; thou art changed, Zenobia, greatly changed, prosperity hath changed thee, the pride of thine heart hath raised thee high, and thou sayest, Who shall bring me down to the ground?

Speak on, said Zenobia, thou wouldst say, I am perverted by gratified ambition, prone to cruelty, fickle, inconstant, treacherous to my friends; thou wilt not give utterance to thy opinion, but I have divined it. In vain she waited his answer, when rising with indignation the meeting was dissolved.

Is not to-morrow the night of the banquet given to the conquering generals, in honour of the taking of Egypt and Bithynia? asked Paulus; verily I had forgotten it, and must return home to make preparations for attending in due splendour on our divine empress.—And I and Longinus accompany thee, added Porphyry, to prepare lyrics on the solemn occasion; farewell, Empress Zenobia, until to-morrow, when we shall kiss the hallowed dust of thy feet —If the choristers of Venus's temple are to assemble at the palace, as I am informed by Caleb, said Hyrcanius, I depart to prepare them.

—Go thou, Orodes, go through the city, commanded Zenobia, as she hastened from the apartment to avoid being left alone with the patriarch; go and proclaim the feast.

O, could Theodosius have foreseen the events of that night, well might he have answered, a feast! rather Palmyrenians sanctify a fast, and cry unto the Lord your God, for the hour of destruction approaches.

The morning dawned, the sun arose, not dimly and in vapour, but bright as Palmyra itself—its gilding beams enlightened the tops of the hills, and fell on the domes and spires of the city—descending, they illumined the terraced roofs of the houses and groves of palms ——those cheering beams, which give joy to the husbandman, rebuke the slumbering idler, inspire with new life the flocks and cattle, and soon drawing away the misty veil of night from the earth, display one universal splendid landscape, glowing with luxuriance and beauty!

With the first blush of morn, the reign of festivity began; the spoils of the conquered provinces were brought forward, and suspended in trophies throughout the city, the houses were ornamented with garlands and banners, the streets thronged with happiness, parties of soldiers strolled negligently through them and the markets, while citizens took their wives and children to the ramparts and fortifications, there with proud importance to explain more than they themselves knew

The public buildings were thrown open; horse, foot, and chariot races began at noon, and the victors were crowned by Zenobia. Zabdas, Timagenes, and the other victorious generals rode in triumph through Palmyra, and behind the chariots walked the captive prisoners of war and their wives and children, all laden with chains. At a window of the palace, which overlooked a spacious part of the city, through which the procession passed, stood Zenobia and her sons.

That custom shall be abolished, remarked the queen, looking with pity upon the guiltless captives; Palmyra shall never again witness a sight like this.—*Palmyra shall never again witness a sight like this*, repeated a voice; she turned, and beheld standing near her Theodosius.

The triumph still passing before them, their eyes became fixed on an empty chariot, the horses of which were led by soldiers on foot; Zenobia looked aside, for it was the chariot of Odenathus, ever used to combat, never for flight. Another followed, and that also was empty, but in magnificence, size, and beauty, it exceeded all the preceding; when arrived before the windows of the palace, the charioteer halted, as if to gratify the queen and those he beheld examining it. This is the superb gift of the wealthy merchant Firmius, said Antiochus; in which the queen shall yet enter Rome in triumph; and he cast an exulting look upon Theodosius.—Yes truly, replied the patriarch, Zenobia, *the queen, may yet, in that chariot, enter Rome in a triumph;* and he walked pensively away.

Evening approaches, and Palmyra and its suburbs become one blaze of light; lamps richly illumine the interior of every dwelling, and at the doors, and on the terraced roofs, are coloured lanthorns displayed, whose fragrant oil diffuse through the air delicious perfume. —Thus the glow-worm shines, betraying itself to the destroying bird of prey.

Every palace is thrown widely open to the invited guests, and that of the queen quickly thronged with those named by Antiochus. A loud burst of cymbals is heard, the organ swells, the tabret sounds, and Zenobia appears. O how glorious, how matchless! in diamond tiara, bracelets, collar, and flowing crimson robes of silk and gold; all eyes are fixed on her beauteous face, watching her grace and excellent majesty.

Orodes, as president of the senate,

arranges the guests, and the feast begins. On the right hand of Zenobia's throne, on beds of gold and silver, sits her father, on her left her children; the generals, in whose honour the banquet is given, clothed in scarlet, and wearing chains of gold, disperse to head the different tables arranged in the same room, whilst at that of the queen are alone assembled chief men of other nations, and the officers of the crown, with their wives and elder sons. The spoils of Egypt, Persia, and Asia Minor, give a brilliancy to the whole, and all is joy and exultation.

Zabdas, rising, holds high the golden bowl, filled with royal wine, and addresses Zenobia, I pour a libation to the gods for the taking of Egypt and Bithynia.—And I, added Victorinus, also rising, for the future conquest of Italy.— Glory to Zenobia, the queen! exclaimed Antiochus.—No longer queen, but empress, added Porphyry, empress of the world: glory to her and our youthful emperors,' who thus for the first time assume their lawful right, the imperial purple, and its attendant prerogatives.

Zenobia rose, Herennianus, Timolaus, and Vaballathus followed her example, and she said to the silent multitude, pointing to the princes, ‘Behold your emperors, the sovereigns of the East, and the future masters of Rome.

A loud and exulting strain of music followed her words, and, Zenobia! Empress of Rome! echoed throughout the palace. One voice alone joined not the otherwise general shout—in one face alone joy gave way to sudden dejection; Orodes dashed from his hand the brimming cup, saying, May I perish ere that hour which gives Palmyra to Rome!— This hour, observed Zenobia, calmly, is that of sunshine, do not thou darken it by ill-timed disaffection; reserve thy opinions until to-morrow, when, at the senate, or in secret, I will hear them.— Consent then, said Orodes, to retain the title of queen, and to reject that of empress.—And by what authority dost thou require it? asked Zenobia, sternly.— Never will *I* acknowledge thee such, said Orodes: upon which she took the jewelled cup that stood before her, saying, Whosoever present refuses to pledge me as Empress of Rome, let him quit the hall. The whole assembly, in a tumult of loyal obedience, obeyed, all excepting Orodes, who left the table.

Thy wilfulness calls for death, said the arbitrary queen, but in consideration of thy age, it is changed to banishment; thou art banished Palmyra. Orodes rushed to her feet, Oh, not so, he cried, say not so, give me death, but let me die in Palmyra.

My word is past, replied Zenobia, and Orodes, scorning further supplication, arose and quitted the hall; Longinus would have followed him, when detained by the queen, who whispering Herennianus, desired him to pursue Orodes and endeavour to calm his mind, by promising in her name a private interview, the ensuing day.

The festivities continued some few hours longer, when, towards their close, turning to Timolaus, Zenobia remarked, as the hour was late, he and his younger brother might retire; the attention of Timolaus otherwise attracted, she fondly touched his cheek to rouse him, when he replied, my mother, I was looking at Theodosius.—At Theodosius! repeated the queen, he is not present, or why not in his place near me, thus purposely left vacant.—He hath been in this room from the beginning, replied Timolaus, wandering through it like a troubled spirit; I have never lost sight of him, and now behold him as if writing with his finger upon the wall, his face turned towards thee, my mother: he looks a Daniel, and this the feast of Belshazzar.

Oh, words of innocence, words inspired by heaven! the countenance of Zenobia, as did that of Belshazzar changed, and her thoughts likewise became troubled, Zenobia also trembled in every limb.—Again she looked up and around, but she no longer saw the patriarch, who, having once met her eye, disappeared:—' Thou art weighed, found wanting, and thy kingdom is give over to' ———. She paused, her heart said, ' The Roman;' but she could not pronounce the word. She rose to retire; again the organ in noble swell gave the signal of prostration, and all at her rising fell to the earth.

But ere they could again rise, a stranger appeared at the entrance, whom Victoria hastening to meet, Zenobia recognized: it was Claudian the Roman.

Gloom and despondency immediately gave place to joy and pleasure at his return, and she rejoiced at being able to receive an account of what was then passing in Italy; again seating herself, she invited him to approach.—And how proceeds Aurelian, with his domestic pretenders to the purple? enquired Zenobia. —They are crushed, Claudian replied.—

And his Goths and Gauls and Scythians? demanded the empress.—They are vanquished, he answered.—On what then, is thy emperor employed? for his active spirit cannot long remain supine; art thou rebuilding the walls of Rome, and establishing new laws and ordinances?—The walls are rebuilt, and its laws are established.—Then say, what will be his next labour? perhaps, she continued, smiling sarcastically, an exepedition to the East.—Even so, replied Claudian; an expedition to the East.

Silence followed; broken at length by Victoria's saying, Answer not the empress thus slow and methodically, dear Claudian, when thou seest it is her wish to know, concerning thy Rome and its master.—What would the queen know? he demanded; again attention became fixed, whilst all present crowded forward, to observe the solemn countenance of the Roman.

Thy intelligence, on arrival from distant parts was wont to flow a copious stream, remarked Zenobia, and not thus ooze from the chilling stone drop by drop?—Bitter waters cannot flow too slowly, replied he, question me, and I will truly answer; forbear to question, and I am silent: but be brief, for I only come hither to fetch my wife Victoria, and may not here abide.—If, said Zenobia, danger result from thy protracted information, instant punishment follows.

Claudian heard, and with generous indignation exclaimed, This the return for my wish to spare thy feelings, by breaking the truth with caution and tenderness! take then, that dreadful truth, O queen! and then judge on whom should punishment fall, on the guiltless messenger, or thy evil advisers.

I see it, said Zenobia, rising in agitation, forgive me, Claudian, I comprehend the purport of thy intelligence; better to restore a part than hazard all; we lose not honour thereby, and it is not yet too late: a friendly embassy shall be dispatched this very hour, and by thee:

Bithynia shall be restored.—Restored! repeated Claudian, dejectedly, it is no longer thine to restore: Bithynia is now Aurelian's; Phrygia, Galatia, Cappadocia, Cilicia; all, all are Aurelian's, and he is marching to Antioch.

To death with that false informer! exclaimed Zabdas, Asia Minor taken, and Antioch threatened, and we not to have heard of it! it cannot be! Where then is now Aurelian himself?—Thou careless shepherd of a slumbering flock! said Claudian, go but a few leagues hence, and thou wilt meet Aurelian; Aurelian is on his way to Palmyra.

A sudden and horrible cry was heard, succeeded by a groan of terror. The words, Aurelian is on his way to Palmyra! spread from mouth to mouth; the dispersing guests fled to their homes; and throughout the city was heard the noise of the whips, the noise of the rattling of the wheels, of the prancing horses, and crash of flying chariots; all in the royal palace was dismay and confusion; until

Zenobia restored peace, when every eye was fixed on her.

Blow the trumpet through the city, she said in a low voice, and call the elders together; light the watch towers of alarm, and be the lamps of joy extinguished.—Victorinus and Balista, do you gather the militia, and here remain captains of the walls! Zabdas thou art my captain; we will see this Aurelian at Antioch.

END OF THE ELEVENTH BOOK.

ZENOBIA,
QUEEN OF PALMYRA.

BOOK XII.

ARGUMENT.

The battle of Imma, Zenobia defeated—Flies to Emessa—Palmyra puts itself in a state of defence—Orodes and others go and consult the oracle of Aphaca, return in despair—Zenobia and her vanquished forces regain Palmyra—Aurelian follows, and the siege begins—Theodosius offers to be the medium towards a restoration of peace—Zabdas returns, and at the gate of Palmyra wounds Aurelian—Zenobia receives a letter from Aurelian, requiring the surrender of the city—Her answer—Theodosius implores her not to send it; he is overruled and thrown into prison—The assault is renewed—Her succours being intercepted, Zenobia leaves Palmyra in the dead of night for Persia—Irenius requests of Elkanah the release of Theodosius—Account of the taking of Zenobia—Palmyra surrenders to Aurelian—The death of Longinus, Zabdas, and Orodes—Aurelian departs for Europe with his royal captive—Zenobia dies.

THE third rising sun saw Zenobia, her elder sons, and their army of one hundred and twenty thousand men, engaged at Imma near Antioch, with the forces of the Roman emperor; the same sun beheld the waters of the Orontes red with Palmyrenian blood, and its banks darkened by rushing flocks of birds of prey.

Hitherto Palmyra had conquered, for it had only fought with soft-limbed Persia and enslaved Egypt; it had now to fight, for the first time, with stern-faced Rome. The vanquished empress, protected by Zabdas, fled back to Antioch; and gathering the scattered remains of her forces, still seventy thousand strong, repaired to Emessa. Aurelian with rapid strides pursued.

There in the plains of Emessa, he encamped his thousands. His Dalmatian and Pannonian horse, his northern legions, his Pretorian bands, troops of Moorish cavalry, the militia of the lately surrendered provinces, and a formidable regiment of Jews, armed with clubs and maces. Dreadful the battle, horrible the carnage: like showers of hail flew darts and javelins, like thunder fell the blows of Jewish weapons upon the brass and iron armour of the Palmyrenians.

a general slaughter followed; the few remaining thousands would have thrown down their arms, when Zenobia, seizing the royal standard of the palm, threw it into the thickest of the enemy, and spurring her courser, plunged after it.

In Palmyra, as yet ignorant of the late events, all was patriotic and enthusiastic ardour; the arsenals were opened and the whole population armed: they did not doubt the success of their cause, and rather rejoiced that Aurelian had thus far penetrated into an hostile country, the inhabitants of which could not fail cutting off his retreat.

Watchmen were placed on all the surrounding heights; fires were never suffered to be a moment extinguished; forges and ovens were constructed; grain brought from the suburbs was secured in the heart of the city, in storehouses purposely erected; timber was felled and given the artificers, who returned it in arrows, bows, and darts; the inhabitants of the neighbouring villages collected their little all, and driving their flocks and herds before them, appeared at the gates, craving admittance; the flocks were penned within the public squares, their forage in the great courts of the temple, and their owners kindly received by the citizens.

Women, and striplings of strength sufficient to draw the bow of defence, were given in charge that part of the town best defended by nature; whilst age and childhood were instructed to collect, and prepare ligatures, bandages, oils, and other necessaries for the wounded.

Intrenchments were thrown up; huge engines of war built, and a strong wall thrown round the aqueduct, by which alone Palmyra was, as yet, supplied with water. One postern only, and that to the East was suffered to be ever opened, and one person only at a time permitted to enter or leave the city.

At the same hour that Zenobia quitted Palmyra to meet the Roman, Antiochus, Hyrcanius, and Orodes left it for Balbec; near that place was the fountain of Aphaca, and to that fountain they repaired to learn the fate of their country; the oblation of linen, silk, and embroidered garments was placed lightly on the waters. Antiochus watched with agonized emotion, Orodes in sullen dejection, but the offering was not accepted, it sank not as their hearts desired: it floated on the surface, and despair and consternation came upon both.

Returning to Palmyra, ere they entered the city, they stood for a few moments on the brow of a southern hill; they looked around, and not a speck appeared in the vast horizon; but ere long, gazing stedfastly towards the north-west, Hyrcanius discerned an object as if a rising cloud; it increased in extent, and as it approached, became darker: it expanded gradually, and assumed the deepest sable hue, conveying dread and horror to the spectator: clouds of dust rolled forward in thick columns, and Orodes, Antiochus and Hyrcanius rushed down the hill to the already opened postern.

The watchmen on the heights, the centinels on the ramparts, the senators assembled on the pinnacles of the temples, the citizens on the terraces of their houses; all, all had seen it, and in an instant the bells of the city tolled; the trumpet and drum had no cessation, and the walls were covered with troops. Every gate of the outer wall was thrown widely open, and the full tide poured forward in torrents,—a mass of blood, and wounds, and slaughter.

Of all the hapless fugitives, one alone retained self-possession, fortitude, and majesty: mounted on a white courser, whose head and neck sparkled with jewels; in one hand her glittering helmet surmounted by thick, but soiled and broken plumes, her javelin red with blood in the other: a battered shield upon her arm, the silken reins of the horse thrown over her neck; she looked around—We went forth thousands strong, and are come back hundreds—but Palmyra still is mine.

And Antioch? exclaimed Paulus.—Gone! she replied, Emessa, Larissa, Arethusa, treasures all, all are gone, or should I be here? O, may this flight of ours, if he pursue, be a snare to bring him to ruin! Zabdas covers our retreat, while the Syrian freebooters, desert Arabs, and others, all join in harassing his rear.

You are not hurt, dear brothers? enquired the young Vaballathus, examining Herennianus and Timolaus.— No, my child, replied his mother, neither have they disgraced their purple: they fought, and had they been opposed to an army of boys, had made that army fly; few of the enemy would exchange blows with these, yet when a coward arm did strike, neither my valiant elder, nor his beauteous brother, ever once hid behind my shield.

At the request of Antiochus, the queen and her sons repaired to the palace, where having laid aside their armour, they partook of refreshment, and retired for short repose. The presence of Zenobia inspired the Palmyrenians with fresh vigour, and the city became impregnable. The next day an early meeting was summoned, which Zenobia attended, clad in the well-known robe of Odenathus; to her jewelled crown was added his crown of laurel, and her soft hand grasped his sword of victory.

Yesterday, she said, was Aurelian's—to-day is mine; in a few hours Balista and I, with our thousands of militia, join Zabdas, and thus will the emperor on every side be hemmed in by enemies. Aurelian no more, I strike the decisive blow, and gathering, in my progress to Europe, a mighty armed mass, pour upon harassed Italy, and conquer declining Rome.

The senate applauded; Empress of Rome! they cried, go and fulfil thy destiny. Scarcely were the words pronounced, than loud and piercing cries were heard, and Orodes suddenly appeared. Aurelian, said he, is in sight, in sight of Palmyra! His close phalanx, his open legion, his engines of destruction, his victorious army of Jews, all are upon us; before him a garden, behind a desert wilderness—the flame and sword his harbingers.

I know his character for rapidity, said Zenobia, astonished, but this exceeds belief. Is it not rather Zabdas returning victorious?

Soon, too soon, alas! the truth was confirmed. Those placed to watch had only proclaimed the appearance of an approaching army, when that army encamped beneath the walls; the pioneers entered on their awful duty, the immediate notice of arrival was given in a shower of darts and stones, which fell like thundering hail upon the roofs and turrets of the city, the Roman shout of war was heard, and the great western brazen gate groaned beneath the strokes of the hostile battering ram.

Are watchmen placed at every gate and postern? asked the queen. Theodosius entering, heard the words—Thy gates are strong, O queen, as the fig-tree until it be shaken. Thus hath the Lord raised up against thee those who scoff at thy embattled walls, and turn thy strong holds into derision. Perhaps I am the only one of this august assembly who is personally known to Aurelian; propose terms of accommodation, and let me be the bearer—offer to restore all thy conquests made within the last three years, to limit Palmyrene to its ancient boundary, and I pledge my life that peace will be the consequence.

Seleucia shall not be surrendered, said Antiochus, for thence the family of the empress derives its origin.—Nor Judea, added Elkanah, for Zenobia, as a sovereign Hebrew of the tribe of Benjamin, has lawful claim to its possession.—Not a furlong of Palmyrene shall be restored, exclaimed Orodes.—Nor a cubit of Egypt gotten by this sword, added Timagenes.

So despotic in wrong, said Theodosius to Zenobia, be despotic in this, and of thyself commission me to go forth without delay, armed with the flag of peace.—It shall be so, said the queen; and turning to Longinus, she directed him to prepare the instrument of conciliation. Longinus with alacrity obeyed, when again the deliberations of the council were interrupted by shouts from without. On enquiry, they were found to proceed from those who witnessed from the walls, a noble and matchless effort of valour.

Although the city was wholly invested with the troops of Aurelian, Zabdas, returned from Emessa with the shattered remains of his brave Palmyrenians, cut through an opposing host, and reached in safety the Syrian gate of Palmyra, where halting, he seized a bow from an archer, and shot an arrow at the pursuing emperor; the weapon entered the side of Aurelian, and a stream of blood flowed over his gilded cuirass. Zabdas, taking advantage of the circumstance, turned upon the appalled enemy with desperate fury, and having beaten them back to their trenches, returned to the city, bearing the Roman standard of the eagle, taken by his own hand.

Hastily entering the council-room, he threw it at the feet of Zenobia, and shewed to all a girdle soaked in blood, which, in the late sally, he had picked up as dropped from the wounded emperor: It is the blood of Aurelian! he said.—Then away with all thoughts of concession, of restoration! exclaimed Zenobia; Aurelian and his powers shall yet be buried in the sands of Palmyra.

New life, new vigour, pervaded every quarter of the city. The siege continued, but not the slightest impression was made on any part of the walls and fortifications, so admirably had they been strengthened by the skill and wisdom of Odenathus: in vain the ramparts were attacked, the battering engines worked, towers and castles erected on the hills to command the walls; ere they could rise to any formidable height, the workmen successively perished in the attempt—machines from the towers of Palmyra poured upon their heads liquid fire and molten lead; engines moved by boys and women, threw darts and stones, whilst Zabdas and the other generals harassed them night and day by repeated excursions into their camp.

The senate of Palmyra became permanent; of the three hundred senators composing it, the half was ever assembled, over whom Zenobia, Herennianus, and his younger brethren, alternately presided, for though the latter were too young to share in the deliberations, their presence inspired awe, and preserved decorum.

Great division existed among the senators, some advising unconditional surrender, others the contrary, whilst a few of the most desperate threatened, ere that should take place, to set fire to the city. Unknown to the queen, six infants were sacrificed to their idols, soothsayers and magicians were consulted, and other cruel impieties committed, which, though they escaped her knowledge, could not that of Theodosius.

Daily, hourly, he still persisted in his first advice to make restitution, to declare her faith, and to attach to her cause the God of truth and justice.—Talk not to me of faith, she replied, whilst besieged by Aurelian; he no more, then will I attend to thee.—Aurelian no more! repeated Theodosius; O that my fears may be groundless!—Canst thou still doubt the event of this contest? returned the queen; his troops slain, those remaining weary, disgusted, mangled, and himself wounded. Whilst she yet spake, a banner of truce arrived, and a noble youth named Marcellus was the bearer of a letter from Aurelian to Zenobia. It was read aloud by the secretary of the senate.

It required her to surrender Palmyra, and promised her and her confederates that they should be allowed to live in plenty and security, in such part of the empire as the Roman senate should appoint; moreover, it demanded the immediate possession of all her treasures, arms, horses, and camels, and the reduction of Palmyra to a free commonwealth.

Turning to Theodosius, the indignant queen appeared to wait his remark on these to her, insolent and unreasonable terms.—Aurelian has proposed his, said the patriarch; do thou propose thine, and through my means, by mutual concession, peace may yet be restored, thy kingdom secured in its full rights as in the happy and glorious reign of Odenathus, and Aurelian induced to withdraw his troops. Concede the conquered provinces, accept their permission to wear the purple, and the Romans will return to the shores of Europe.

This is thy opinion? observed Zenobia.—And mine! exclaimed Orodes, but a third voice was not heard, and a murmur of discontent arose, when Zenobia ordered Longinus to write what she should dictate. Fearful that she was adopting the advice of Theodosius and Orodes, all present listened with sullen gloom; but soon this gloom gave place to applause and admiration, and at every sentence, Paulus and Porphyry, Antiochus and Elkanah, Valerius and Victorinus, expressed with enthusiasm, their decided approbation of the answer.

'Zenobia, Empress of the East, to the Roman Emperor Aurelian.—No man except thyself, durst demand of me what thy letter requires: it is not by letters, but by valour I can be induced to submit. Cleopatra died rather than yield to Octavius, and shall Zenobia do less? I daily expect succours from Persia, Arabia, and Armenia—all are hastening to my relief; what then will become of thee and thy vagrant armies, whom the robbers of Syria have already put to flight? Then wilt thou lay aside that pride and presumption with which thou callest on me to surrender, as if thou wert the conqueror of the universe.'

She ceased—A glorious declaration! exclaimed the senate, tumultuously.—The spirit of Cleopatra lives in thee, my daughter said Antiochus.—It is an answer worthy the Queen of great Palmyra, remarked Elkanah. And Longinus, in silence, having folded and sealed the letter, placed it in a crimson bag, and delivered it to the messenger, when Theodosius, rapidly ascending a few steps of the throne, laid his hand on the arm of Zenobia.

Send it not, he cried, O send it not!—Be it dispatched at the instant, returned Zenobia, rudely shaking off his hand.—Queen, he still repeated, with fervour, yet hear me—hear my objections; but one moment, one moment's delay is all I ask.—Another word, returned the empress, and I shall treat thee not as the apostle of the Christians, but as the spy of the Romans.

Theodosius retreated, and stood apart; the queen from her elevated throne, the seated elders around, looked upon him, surveying the stern dignity of his appearance. Then, said he, armed with a firm and intrepid air, I shake the dust of Palmyra from my feet—I shake it off, Zenobia, as thou shookest from thee this hand, by which thou wert to have been baptized.

Baptized! exclaimed a multitude of voices; Zenobia to have embraced baptism! our empress a Christian!—Speak, said Theodosius; thou art called upon, and answer the question.—The faith of my people is my faith, she replied.—And can the proud Zenobia stoop to equivocation? Thy people are of every faith, but of what faith art thou?—If of Christian, said Antiochus, let Aurelian with my free will enter Palmyra.—If Zenobia own herself a Nazarite, added Elkanah, I will myself open the gate to the Roman.

Thy silence, queen, remarked Paulus, confirms the words of this man; if false, let him take heed—the age of martyrdom is not passed.—Nor that of apostacy, returned the patriarch; behold the pattern in thyself. Answer then, Zenobia, what faith doth thou profess? The storm is come upon thee, O beloved queen, but let adversity confirm thy faith.—If she confesses to the name of Jesus, said Elkanah, I raise the city, and call in Aurelian.—Confess it, and call God to the defence of thy city, returned Theodosius.

Banish that seditious Christian, exclaimed the heads of the council, or we are freed from all allegiance to thee, O queen! Banish him, thrust him out of Palmyra! imprison, stone him! Elkanah had spread the word, and the doors were at that instant burst open by a furious multitude, who vociferated, We are the voice of Palmyra. To death with the Christians! they have sold us to Rome. Drag this their ruler from the presence, and behead him.

Zenobia, though pale and agitated, resented their rebellious violence, and rising, ordered the hall to be cleared, and the doors fastened; then addressing the patriarch, Away, she said, away, whilst thou art yet safe! Go to thy friend, the Roman, or my power may not be sufficient to save thee from danger. Give him a guard and passports to the emperor's camp.—I accept them not, replied the patriarch, firmly; thy fate is come, and I will not leave thee. Oh, wretched queen! I am safe; it is thou that art surrounded by danger: avert it, in pity to thyself and empire, avert it—look upon these disaffected hundreds, and strengthened by divine power, own thyself a disciple of Christ.

Away! repeated Zenobia, angrily, nor thus persist in provoking their wrath on thy head and mine.—Am I to consider this an abjuration of thy new belief? he demanded. Dost thou, by these equivocating words, really deny the name of Jesus?—Again she was silent, when he continued, The civil punishment of apostacy is confiscation of goods—the divine punishment on sovereigns may be confiscation of kingdom.—Farewell.

He was quitting the hall, when he perceived standing at the door, the messenger who had received Zenobia's letter in charge, and who, purposely or negligently, attentive to all that had passed, had not yet departed. Theodosius, instantly returning, exclaimed with joyful tenderness, Oh, merciful heaven, thy hand is in this! the letter is not yet gone, and all may be saved; now Zenobia hear me—though thou hast dishonoured thy profession, it is the duty of a Christian to endeavour to preserve thee and this hapless city; recal this thy letter, for hast thou not remarked the imprudence, the inadvertency thou hast committed in ——

This man talks much, interrupted Porphyry, and his censure of the letter is most unreasonable, for in brevity, force, wit, and firmness, it hath never been surpassed.—A most admirable composition, repeated several of the senators.— Exquisitely worded, said Paulus.—It was a fair answer to Aurelian's insolent demand, observed Longinus; and the latter sentence decided the fate of the letter: Caleb, snatching the bag containing it, from the tardy messenger, darted from the room, and sent it without delay to the camp.

Oh blindness and infatuation! exclaimed Theodosius, when silence again prevailed; hear me once more.—Thou shalt not be heard, returned the queen, inspired with boundless arrogance by the adulation of those around her; none shall hear thee, and on another sentence coming from thy lips, thou art snatched for ever from my presence, and thrown into confinement, for I now begin to regard thee as a mover of sedition, a perverter of all good, and an enemy to Palmyra.

She ceased, and Elkanah watched the lips of Theodosius to hear that other sentence, nor long did he watch; Theodosius spake; and those habituated to obey the looks of the queen, instantly surrounded and seized him: had Zenobia's command been strictly obeyed, he would only have been confined to the Christian college, but as it was Elkanah and his dependants that conducted Theodosius from the hall, he was thrown into the common dungeon of the public prison.

Hast thou any message to the empress? asked the insulting Elkanah.—Yes, said the patriarch, with calm dignity, still tell her to beware of evil counsellors, and remember Ahab's prophets. Elkanah left the place with the scowl of derision, and on his return to the hall, being questioned by Zenobia, was silent, but the person who had accompanied him repeated the words of Theodosius, and Zenobia trembled; she well remembered the advice of Theodosius, to make the death of Ahab her study, and it had become familiar to her. Release the patriarch, said the queen; then, to Longinus, is the letter gone?—It is, and Aurelian has recommenced the assault.

Wretched Zenobia! thou art fallen,

for ever art thou fallen! when thou orderedst profane hands to seize the person of a faithful witness, then fell thyself, thy empire: hadst thou but timely checked thy vehemence, abated thy pride, listened to the voice of reason, accepted the mediation, given thyself up to the advice of an upright minister, that holy man would have exposed the folly of thy rash and ill-judged answer.

Theodosius, his judgment unbiassed by worldly motives, his passions calmly regulated, alone saw the error thou wert committing, an error overlooked by three hundred senators famed for wisdom; an error which escaped the penetration of all thy learned counsellors, that of imprudently acquainting Aurelian that succours *were* expected by Palmyra—will he not take advantage of the information? Oh, Zenobia, he has; thy letter was no sooner read than Aurelian forgot his wound, and with all the rapidity of military ardour directed thy expected supplies to be intercepted; they were indeed coming from Persia, Armenia, and Arabia, and had they reached Palmyra (a safe passage opened for them by Zabdas), it would have been saved; but now all hope is cut off; no succour now will reach Palmyra! Ere the receipt of thy answer to a letter designed only to intimidate thee, it was the intention of Aurelian to raise the siege as hopeless, and with the accustomed pretence of retiring to quell distant rebellion, he had for ever quitted Asia; but when, guided by learned rabbis, invincible generals, and sublime and enlightened heathens, thou in evil hour abjuredst the gospel, in outward act if not in heart, and ungratefully dismissed thy faithful adviser, thou didst seal the fate of thy country and thyself.

Art thou waiting from day to day for these friendly succours? are thy own supplies at length exhausted by this long protracted siege?—A prisoner is taken, and brought before the senate, from whom they learn that Saracens, Armenians, and Persians have all been either intimidated, seduced to return, or on refusal defeated by Aurelian.

This is a fatal blow! said Orodes; how could so palpable an error have escaped us!—A more fatal blow than even that, cried Zabdas, entering hastily, has been struck; the enemy has turned the course of the acqueduct, and our only supply of water is thus cut off.

Then did the heart of Zenobia faint, the pride of the sovereign was no longer seen, the Amazonian character wholly vanished—and what remained? —a timid, helpless, forlorn, and fainting, woman.

When recovered, This, she said, is the final stroke! deprived of water, for a few days only, under this burning sun— the city thus crowded with inhabitants, flocks, herds, and cattle, it becomes a scene of pestilence, of death, one universal grave—a charnel house. Succour must be had, and from without—from Persia it can only come.

And from Persia it would be instantly

afforded, said Longinus, Sapor being the sworn enemy to Rome.—But who can escape thither, who if they could would rush on certain death in making the attempt? asked Antiochus.—I, said Zabdas, for my life is Palmyra's.—Then preserve it, returned Zenobia, for the sake of Palmyra; and she took Orodes apart, and conferred with him; astonishment appeared in his looks; he shortly after quitted her, when turning, she addressed the assembly——

In times of peace, wonderous events are scattered through years; in times of war, crowded into as many days: three of importance are come to my knowledge within the last hour—Egypt is retaken, and convoys of provisions from every part of this ungrateful land hourly arrive in the camp of Aurelian; but to counterbalance these disastrous events, learn that Sapor is dead, and that his son Hormisdas reigns; having been brought up under Orosanga, the Persian captive, whose life was spared by Odenathus, Hormisdas is the friend of Palmyra. He hath heard of our danger, and is hastening to our relief; his thousands on the eastern banks of the Euphrates only wait my call. I now leave you for a few moments, remain at your posts, nor let me find one missing at the return of Orodes; continue your deliberations, but take no further steps respecting the garrison until ye see me again.

Accompanied by Victoria, and attended by Terentia and Mariam, purposely selected on the occasion, Zenobia quitted the palace, and went towards New Zaantha, where lay buried Septimia. Make firm your torches in the earth, said the queen, and remove the stone from the mouth of the sepulchre; they obeyed, but their united strength could only leave a small aperture, at which Zenobia entered with a torch, whilst they remained without.

Nor tear was shed, nor sigh breathed by Zenobia, as she raised for the last time the covering thrown over the embalmed features of that beloved one, and long looked upon them—I regretted thee my mother, O blessed be God that thou didst not live to see this hour! and bestowing one last kiss, she softly let fall the drapery and hastened from the spot.

From the sepulchre of Septimia, she passed to that of Odenathus; here also leaving her attendants at the door, she entering shut it after her, thus enclosing herself with the remains of him now more than ever lamented. Hadst thou been living, said Zenobia, prostrating herself on his tomb, this hour had never come, I had not suffered, I had not fallen! then raising herself, she approached his beauteous bending statue, now in appearance mourning over his dear, his lost Zenobia; sighs and tears were no longer supprest, in an agony of grief she clasped the cold marble to her throbbing bosom, rested her head upon its shoulder, looked in its expressive face, almost fancying it returned her look, and sobbed in anguish, fondly hanging upon it.

Her torch in one hand, and her veil,

which concealed her face, in the other, Zenobia left the tomb, and still followed by her faithful friends, returned to the palace. She next repaired to the apartments of her sons; Herennianus alone was awake, Timolaus and Vaballathus slept the deep sleep of health and innocence; stooping, she kissed them; and then went to her elder, who of an age to understand what passed around, him, fell weeping on the breast of Zenobia, as she sat by the side of his bed.

Where is Theodosius, my mother, asked the youth,—if evil has befallen him I renounce comfort.—Theodosius, my child, is at the Christian college, safe and unharmed of me.—Have I then thy permission to seek him there, to abide with him at that place, or bring him back to the palace?—Not now, replied Zenobia, this is the hour of repose; rest thee then, dear child, this night, and to-morrow thou mayest join him—good night, Herennianus, sleep in peace, and forget not in thy prayers to God, thy hapless mother.

On her return to the senate, the members of which had not quitted their seats during her absence, she enquired for Orodes.—He is not yet come back, said Antiochus. And she continued leaning pensively and in silence upon the arm of her couch: no one spake, all was doubt and suspense, for none knew her intentions, and no one dared question her; when Orodes again appeared.

Thy orders are fulfilled, said he, and every thing arranged. Zenobia came forward, and the whole assembly in astonishment arose, looking alternately on Orodes and the empress. Turning to where stood the amazed Antiochus, she embraced him, saying, Farewell, my father, I go myself to Persia, to bring back succours.

Cries and lamentations was the answer of all, who, crowding to the doors, intercepted her passage.—Oh, not so! Zenobia, exclaimed Antiochus, rather submit to Rome than hazard thy adored person; security alone is within these walls, every step beyond them is danger; send thither, but do not go thyself, for shouldst thou be taken, shouldst thou be killed—oh, my child, nor I, nor Palmyra can outlive thee.

What number of camels hast thou ordered? asked Zenobia of Orodes; Five only replied he, I feared a greater escort might create confusion and betray us: Victorinus and I attend thee, a fleet dromedary is for thee prepared, and two horses laden with gold and jewels, presents to Hormisdas. It is now midnight; we may reach the Euphrates by to-morrow, and Ctesiphon where the king at this time resides, the next morn, if he is not already with his army, set out to meet us. In four days we may, therefore, promise to return to Palmyra, not as thus; few in number stealing away in the dead of night, but at the head of a great and powerful Persian host, abundantly supplied: on the fifth day we shall see Aurelian raise the siege.

A warm and ample cloak was thrown

over Zenobia's person, and she once more bade Antiochus farewell. To a few of the senators she gave her hand, and then conducted by Orodes, Longinus, Zabdas, and Victorinus, left the hall.

A multitude of nobles and officers, seizing lighted torches, followed her to the outer gate of the palace, where stood the prepared escort: she was placed on the dromedary, the rest mounted their camels and horses, and they passed silently through the streets accompanied by hundreds on foot.

When reached the outer wall they stopped and listened with eager caution: the centinels having been prepared, opened the gate without noise, but though the night was dark, fearful of discovery, each was forced to extinguish his lamp and torch.

Caleb was the first who went out at the gate, he walked to and fro to examine that all was clear; then returned and whispered Orodes, himself and train approached the empress, and surrounded her closely on all sides; at every instant they stopped and became motionless; the watchmen on the towers and ramparts, continued their accustomed cries; the soldiers still challenged, and the trumpet at intervals sounded; the party of fugitives went forward, whilst the gate behind was still kept open though guarded by Zabdas with a strong detachment, ready, if necessary, to clear a passage back.

Not a breath was heard, nor the sound of a step; they passed in safety the last wall, they took a circuit to avoid the camp of the enemy, and ascended the western hill, when a sudden crash created dread and alarm: passing through a sloping vineyard, one of the camels stumbled, and several heavy loose stones rolled down into the valley upon the tents of the Romans; they stopped and listened, all was again silent.

I hail the omen, whispered Orodes, we cover our enemies with dust and confusion, and they quickened their pace;

once past the salt marshes, they galloped onward, and having reached the plains beyond them, they darted forward and continued their course with the utmost speed.

At the instant they thus set off, Caleb returned alone to the city, and as he re-entered it, cried in a smothered enraptured voice, Now close the gate, and bless your gods, for Zenobia is safe.

What is thy purpose, my nephew? asked Elkanah of Herennianus, in bringing this man a third time before me: What, and who is he?—I have already informed thee more than once, answered the youthful prince, but thou wouldst not listen to me, it is Irenius the pastor of Palmyra, come, in the name of his Christian brethren, to implore the release of their patriarch Theodosius.

He was imprisoned by order of the empress, observed Elkanah.—But by a subsequent order was released, replied the youth; here are the names of ninety senators who heard the words of my empress mother, ordering him to be set at liberty, and in her name, in that of my brother Timolaus, and my own, I now require, that Theodosius be brought before me, for I have sought him at the college, and sought in vain; if thou dost still refuse to produce him, my uncle, I charge thee with his death.

Go to your homes my industrious citizen-friends, said Elkanah to Irenius and his brethren, nor thus idly waste your time in sauntering through palaces.

Would that every Christian were banished Palmyra! remarked Hyrcanius, who, with Caleb, was standing near the table, at which Elkanah was writing, and that the whole sect were beyond these walls; for they do but consume our provisions, without rendering effectual service in the hour of fight.

Elkanah continued writing, and on Irenius mildly pressing him for an answer respecting the patriarch, he at length offered him the parchment he had even now filled up before the eyes of all; and which had been given to him by Zenobia, on his departure for Judea, for the purpose of recalling the Jews, and raising supplies towards the rebuilding of the temple.

Whose is this signature, and whose this seal? demanded Elkanah, — on Irenius replying they were those of the empress, he added, then read her order for the banishment of every Christian from Palmyra.—It cannot be, interrupted the prince, for when Theodosius applied for their removal, my mother resolutely opposed it: moreover this cannot be her will, since we saw thee take a blank roll and write thereon: this is thy edict, not that of the empress.

It is her seal and signature, replied Elkanah; then rising, he deliberately gathered together his scattered papers, saying to Caleb: Do thou see the order executed, and if necessary call in force;

every Christian found in this city after the sixth hour, suffers death.

It shall not be! exclaimed the prince, this, thy command, shall not be obeyed unauthorised by the senate; none of the senators consulted thereupon! not even apprized! retract this edict, my uncle, or I instantly assemble a council, and make known to it thy violent proceedings. — Obey, said Elkanah to Caleb; but Caleb, who knew that the authority of Elkanah must fade before that of the young emperor, coolly retreated, saying, I would wish any other than myself selected to execute this thy will.

I appeal to the great lords Antiochus and Paulus, said Irenius, emboldened by the protection of Herennianus, the murmurs of Caleb, and the silence of Hyrcanius; I appeal to them.—Fetch hither the great lords Antiochus and Paulus, repeated Elkanah to Caleb, who, without hesitation flew to obey, hoping from them a milder sentence; they, with others, the same moment came, and without hesitation, confirmed that sentence passed by Elkanah.

There will be many hundreds less to feed, observed Paulus, as he indolently reclined at his length upon a golden couch of down, and with negligence glanced at the whole person of Irenius. Some hundred scions of Christianity, added Porphyry, carelessly turning over the leaves of a book which lay upon the table, at which he stood, will make a goodly plantation in Italy, in the place of those rooted up in the late ninth persecution.—Would that they had been transplanted thither years back, exclaimed Antiochus, hastily traversing the room, 'then had Zenobia never heard the name of Christian.'

' Shall any more of the great lords be summoned? asked Elkanah, who still continued tying up papers and parchments in separate rolls.—Irenius raised his meek eyes to heaven, and then enquired; were they permitted to take with them their effects, whilst the prince, bursting into tears, caught the robe of Antiochus, and entreated to be brought to Theodosius.

Thus were all present situated, when a loud and appalling noise was heard without, and an armed multitude furiously entered the house, spreading themselves through every apartment. Where is that traitor, Elkanah! exclaimed a voice louder than the rest, and Zabdas, with drawn sword and eyes darting fire, rushed in followed by a concourse of people.

Are folly and idiotism ever to govern our deliberations! what is this edict that Caleb tells me thou hast issued.—To send the Christians to Aurelian! Wherefore, then was the flight of the empress kept thus profoundly secret! Wouldst thou have her return intercepted, as were the expected supplies? Thy counsel, man, has done much mischief in Palmyra, and as already the Christians are arming to rescue their patriarch, I demand of thee his instant release.—

This is our Sabbath, replied Elkanah, slowly retiring from the room with his papers, and I never transact business on the Sabbath-day.

Be comforted, dear prince, said Zabdas, addressing Herennianus, the prisons of Palmyra shall be examined, and Theodosius restored to thee, and should our search prove fruitless, Elkanah will, ere long, be compelled to own where he has caused the patriarch to be secreted, for we now hourly look for the return of thy royal mother.

A loud laugh of derision followed the words of Zabdas, which, on looking around, to his indignant amazement, he saw proceeded from a Roman officer taken prisoner by Balista a few minutes before in a desperate sally from the walls.

On Zabdas enquiring the cause: Didst thou not say, that Palmyra hourly looked for the return of her empress? asked the officer.—Dost thou insult me, Roman! Zabdas fiercely cried.—Pardon me, Palmyrenian, answered the other, the laugh at thy ignorance was involuntary, for I would not willingly insult the unfortunate.—The unfortunate! repeated the general.—Yes, truly; art thou not justly termed thus, having lost the miracle of nature, a being I gazed on until my eyes were dazzled, a woman whose equal is not to be found in Rome; nay, on the earth!

All present stood transfixed and silent, struck with horror at a suspicion, which came like fire upon the brain.—Instant freedom, said Zabdas, without ransom is thine, so thou conceal nothing from me.—The Roman gratefully accepted the conditions, and was preparing to comply, when suddenly checking himself, he pointed to the gathering multitude, who now eagerly crowded into the apartments and pressed upon him, saying, They will tear me in pieces.

Zabdas for answer, presented him his own unsheathed sword, and extended his right hand, which the Roman grasped, and as he grasped it firmly, added in haste, Zenobia's taken.

Universal silence followed, and the officer letting fall the hand of Zabdas, felt at that awful moment more a Palmyrenian than a Roman. In the accents of sensibility and delicate tenderness, he continued,

She is at this moment the prisoner of Aurelian. Heard ye not the exulting shouts which proclaimed the important capture? Her escape from the city was discovered by some 'loose stones falling from the brow of the vineyard-hills, a few of which struck full upon the tent of Aurelian, and woke him. I was one of fifty light-horse sent at the same instant by the emperor in pursuit. Fearful that relief unknown to us might rescue her from our arm, we suffered her to reach the Euphrates, on the opposite banks of which we distinguished encamped a Persian army, and which was headed by the son of the satrap, Orosanga, the firmest friend of Palmyra; had Zenobia once crossed the river, all was her own, and already were boats prepared to take her over.

A brave man who accompanied the queen, dismounted, and leaped into that nearest the edge of the water, whilst another, more aged, assisted her to alight. She looked to the opposite bank, and there distinguished, mounted on an armed elephant, Hormisdas, the youthful king, surrounded by his friendly thousands. O the transport of that look! for I beheld it. She saw she was recognised,

their cheering acclamations of welcome, and with a loud cry of gratitude and delight, sprang upon a low rock with intent to descend from thence into the boat; in the eagerness of the moment, her helmet fell to the ground, and her cloak dropped off. Such the effect of this sudden, this first sight of your Zenobia, that our soldiers, forgetting their ambuscade, expressed their feelings in a murmur of wonder and admiration. The Palmyrenian who was already in the boat, looked fearfully around, as did the queen and those of her train; but silence being again restored, he placed one foot upon the edge, and catching hold of the branch of a tree with the right hand to keep the boat firm, stretched out the other to assist her.

Not the hand of the Palmyrenian seized the extended hand of Zenobia, continued the officer, looking down with pleasure upon his own; mine seized hers. Aurelian! was the loud cry of war; and forth from behind the rocks appeared our fifty armed men; whilst they put all of her train that resisted to the sword, and bound the remainder, I secured my glorious prize. Already prepared with a close litter, we fastened it on the back of the dromedary, and our speed was swift as the winds. I repeat to thee, General, Zenobia is a prisoner in the camp of Aurelian; and now perform thy promise—give me freedom.

O unnecessary demand! look, soldier, look at the effects of thy narration. Who now thinks of thee, or of a thousand such? What now prevents thy return to freedom? Every gate in Palmyra is thrown widely open, and to the utter confusion and astonishment of the enemy, the Roman camp is the same hour filled with a Palmyrenian population of six hundred thousand souls.

Unarmed, defenceless, Pagans, Jews, Christians, men, women, and children, pour from the gates, creep through the posterns, leap from the walls, drop from the watch-towers, and rush to the camp of Aurelian; they clear the entrenchments, climb the palisades, strive to enter the tents, hang upon the armed soldier, embrace his knees, and the loud, and universal, and lamentable cry is, Our queen! our queen! Zenobia, our queen! Not a Roman heart but is moved with amazement and compassion.

This was indeed the mother of her people! remarked the youthful general,

Marcellus. But fear not, ye Palmyrenians, for the word of the emperor is past, and the life of Zenobia spared. Before her capture, he threatened to lay your city in ashes; but one sight of your young and beauteous queen has wrought in him a wondrous change, and he now swears that not a stone of it shall be removed: your treasures he would also leave you, had he the power, but they are not his to dispose of—they appertain as the spoils of war to his soldiers; your lives and private wealth are alone secured to you.

Take all, they cried; strip every temple, every palace, every dwelling, but restore to us our queen.—Never, replied Marcellus; therefore hope it not. Should thy queen be given to you again, though we strip Palmyra to a shell, yet would it in a few years regain its grandeur and presumption; again would it brave Rome, and talk of joining ' Europe, a goodly field, to its Asiatic garden.' You will see Zenobia no more, for as the victim due to

the insulted eagle, she is doomed to suffer.
—Suffer! exclaimed they.—Not death,
replied Marcellus, but the loss of freedom: she must live to adorn the triumph of Aurelian.

Those who heard this dreadful sentence, fell upon the earth in utter despair; the sands around were wetted with tears, and scattered with torn hair and rended garments, whilst the air was filled with grief and bewailing cries.

The Roman legions, led on by their commanders, entered the open and deserted gates of Palmyra, and unmolested, proceeded through its empty streets and squares to collect the spoils. Thus was Palmyra in a short time filled with Romans, and the Roman camp with Palmyrenians. In vain were repeated orders sent from Aurelian's tent to the inhabitants, enjoining them to go back to the city and protect their houses, and observe that his soldiers conformed strictly to their directions; they heard all unheeded. Perceiving Claudian come forth, and conduct his wife, the weeping Victoria, to a tent in the centre of the camp adjoining that which they were told was Aurelian's (followed by Sabina, Mariam, and Terentia); they thronged thither, but were prevented by a powerful cohort which guarded it, from approaching nearer; they then threw themselves upon the ground, and stretching out their hands, still continued imploring to be allowed one sight of her.

In pity to yourselves, keep off, said Claudian, returning from the tent in which he had left Victoria and the other females; if any attempt violence or a rescue, the soldiers who guard the queen, are charged by Aurelian to put her to instant death: one stands over her even while I now speak, with a drawn sword, and but awaits the signal to deprive her of life.

But dost thou not deceive us? demanded they. Is she really living?—She is, but from the hour that she was seized at the Euphrates to this, has not opened her lips, or scarcely unclosed her eyes. Aurelian has seen her, but she has seen no one.—Many other questions were put by the Palmyrenians to Claudian, but neither Antiochus nor Elkanah, who both stood near, asked any.

Whither art thou going, most worthy prelate? enquired Porphyry of Paulus, whom he perceived leisurely mounting a camel held by his servants, near one of the gates of the city.—To the West, replied Paulus, for the sandy air of this Palmyra having become insufferably heated by the late over-crowding of its inhabitants, I sigh for Antioch, its fragrant baths, and luscious fruits. Wilt thou, my friend, go with me thither?

Willingly, replied Porphyry, for *I* do not find the tumult of a besieged city so congenial to study and meditation, as did the philosopher of Syracuse; and from Antioch I proceed to Tyre, being anxious to learn how my scribes have proceeded in my absence, and to deliver to them these my late writings in Palmyra, in order to have copies for dissemination through Italy.

Here is Longinus, said Paulus; let us meet him, and propose the journey. And when Longinus approached, leading Herennianus and Timolaus in each hand, Paulus addressed him.—Do you forget, Longinus coolly asked, that I am secretary to the queen, a senator of Palmyra, and governor to these princes?—The bishop and the Tyrian pressed no further, but proceeded on their way, yet ere they departed, looked with disdain and indifference over their shoulders, and watched the faithful Athenian, who continued walking with his illustrious pupils towards the Roman camp.

Arrived before the tent of the royal captive, Herennianus, disengaging himself from Longinus, darted towards it, whilst Timolaus, unable to get free, cried in piteous accents, O suffer me to see my mother! Longinus at length released him, in the hope that their beauty, innocence, and distress, would prevail over the guards, and gain them admission; but by the guards they were both tenderly repulsed, yet still they persisted in their design to burst their way to Zenobia's tent, when from it came a Roman of warlike stature and fierce aspect.

He stopped, and turned with haughty indignation upon the princes. Strip them of their purple, he cried to the attendant soldiers, which order was instantly obeyed, and the imperial robes detached from their beauteous forms, were fastened to the glittering standards of the eagle planted before the regal tent.

Longinus looked upon the Roman— his lofty crest, his golden inlaid helmet, his highly-wrought breast-plate, and ample and effulgent shield—in one hand grasping a long and ponderous javelin, in the other a blood-stained two-edged sword—Is it Aurelian? asked Longinus of Marcellus, who stood near.—No, replied the general, in a low voice; it is Sandarion, tribune of the tenth cohort, and one most in favour with the emperor.

Who are these? enquired the rough Sandarion, pointing to the princes. Am I not right, in supposing them the sons of thy Zenobia?—Thou art, replied Longinus; these two blameless and lovely children, and that third in the arms of its grandfather, are the offspring of the virtuous Odenathus, who, when living, was the best friend of Rome.

By the command of the tribune, the youths were immediately seized by the soldiers, and Vaballathus torn from the convulsive grasp of Antiochus.

And who art thou thyself? demanded Sandarion. The queen's secretary, replied Longinus. Sandarion paused, and looked stedfastly upon him; then, with a look and accent full of meaning, Secretaries, he said, write letters —That most assuredly is their usual employment, answered the Athenian, calmly.—The emperor, some few days back, received a letter from this Syrian queen, this Zenobia; but perhaps thou wert ignorant of its contents.—I could not be ignorant, since it was written by me, Longinus replied.—Thou didst write that letter?—I did.—A letter in which the Roman power was braved, and its emperor personally insulted, repeated Sandarion.—I wrote it, signed, sealed, and dispatched it, answered Longinus.—And thy wisdom could not foresee the consequences? remarked the fierce Sandarion, contemptuously. What is thy name?—Longinus.

Longinus! repeated Sandarion, and contempt and ferocity vanished from his countenance.—This! exclaimed Marcellus in wonder, this the Longinus whose writings are the admiration of our country and the glory and boast of Greece!—The same, said Claudian, advancing, O Longinus, how couldst thou have suffered Zenobia, or been thyself betrayed into such flagrant error as that letter discovers; where was thy judgment wandering? but for that, we should not have known that Palmyra expected supplies; ere the receipt of that answer to Aurelian, we had private orders from him to raise the siege.

At this heart-wounding intelligence, the face of Longinus underwent great change. I wrote the letter, at length he calmly replied.—I would advise thee, said Sandarion, to conceal that thou wert the writer; when questioned by the emperor, make it appear the production of thy scribes, who, beneath the vengeance of Aurelian, may escape with life.

Not though death were immediately to follow the avowal, returned Longinus, firmly.—Be assured that death will follow it, said Claudian; for though the queen hath by a sign acknowledged that she dictated it, the man whose hand-writing it is, appears one of the first on the fatal list of proscription: be therefore advised, and escape whilst yet in thy power. I will hereafter glory to the emperor that I thus counselled thee, nay, aided thee to elude his severity.—And I, repeated Marcellus —And I, said Sandarion.

Perceiving that he stirred not, Marcellus and Claudian renewed their entreaties, and on a message being delivered to them, added, We are summoned by the emperor; go then, noble, excellent Longinus—go, nor brave thy fate. They went towards the tent of Aurelian, following Sandarion, who led the princes, and as they entered, looked back to see whether Longinus had complied with their advice, when, with undissembled regret, they found him close at their side.

Again Claudian and Marcellus stopped, and spread across the entrance their ample cloaks to hide him from view, when, putting them aside, Longinus pointed to the children, saying, Those princes were given in trust to me by their royal mother, and duty bids me follow them even to death. The Romans could no longer oppose his entrance, and the door of the tent was closed.

Night approached, and the enemy having brought out of the city treasures inexhaustible, piled them in the surrounding plains: gold, precious stones, embroidered curtains and garments, rich stuffs, pearls, and spices—horses, camels, and waggons were laden with such; the spoils of the temples were next displayed, and lastly, the royal camels, elephants, and chariots.

Nor spoils nor treasures were regarded by the Palmyrenians as objects of regret, but when they beheld among the chariots, that of Odenathus, never entered but by him, and that of Zenobia, built by Firmius, which she had not yet ascended, they burst into pitiable cries and lamentations—they hung upon the wheels, they caught the traces, clung to the well-known horses (favourites of Odenathus), and exclaimed to the Roman troops, O leave us these! But lamentation soon ceased, when universal attention was the same moment attracted to one distant spot.

From the tent of Aurelian came a numerous party of soldiers, whose ranks opening, discovered in the centre, a man stripped of his upper garment, bareheaded, and with neck uncovered, as prepared for death.

Halt! cried Sandarion, their leader; here, in the front of the captive Zenobia's tent, strike off his head.—Who and what is he? enquired the Palmyrenians, as they crowded to the place.—O not so! shrieked Herennianus and Timolaus, rushing from the royal tent, and clinging round the victim—not so! O spare his life, for we love him.—Ye gods! exclaimed a senator, bursting through the crowd, can it be Longinus!

He would have penetrated to the fatal spot, when Sandarion commanded his troops to form a wide circle, and suffer no Palmyrenian to enter it. Thus kept far distant, they could only at first distinguish the manly form of Longinus as he appeared addressing the Romans. He seemed to be persisting in one firm assertion, and frequently extended his right hand, which hand they beheld Sandarion, Marcellus, and Claudian take alternately, as in friendship and condolence.

Longinus, after a few minutes conversation with each, stooped to the princes, who still fondly clung to him, and seemed as bidding them farewell, and giving them instructions. Once more erect, his whole deportment calm and dignified, the expression of his smile angelic, that of his look sublime, he turned his face upon the tent where was Zenobia confined; his left hand stretched towards that tent, the other on his heart, he stood the emblem of truth and fidelity. Sandarion went behind him—Marcellus and Claudian averted their heads, wrapping them in their cloaks; the centurion gave the signal, and the same moment the royal youths were covered with the blood of Longinus.

Bring forth the other dead, cried Sandarion, and place them with this, that their friends may recognize and remove them for interment. Aurelian now sits in judgment, and this is the valley of death. — Several bodies were conveyed into the circle by a troop of barbarians, who, on flinging them down, shouted and wildly clapped their hands in exultation; many, more savage than the rest, would have proceeded to wanton indignities, had not the generous Romans interfered, and driven them away.

Who shall be next killed? asked a terrific Moor. — Thou, returned Claudian, if thou presumest to touch one not doomed by the emperor. Approach, ye Palmyrenians — come and mourn over these, executed by order of Aurelian: here lie breathless above two hundred bodies, four-score of whom were, when living, the most esteemed of Zenobia's ministers. Antiochus, thou wert on the list, but the pleadings of thy grandsons preserved thee; that dreadful list is full, and vengeance is satisfied. Hark to the sound of that clarion—all who hear that sound are, by the oath of Aurelian, secure of life.

Thanks, gracious heaven! exclaimed a feeble, aged voice, and from among the prostrate Christians arose one thus providentially saved. The venerable Artabazus, who, conscious that his name was on the awful scroll as one of the queen's senators, had been prevailed upon by Irenius to conceal himself among their number, every Christian being, by the order of Aurelian, assured of life and protection.

Whilst the Palmyrenians hastened from all parts to examine the bodies of the murdered, and to select those of their relatives and friends, in order to remove them to a place of security for that night (for already troops of jackalls, vultures, and other beasts and birds of prey appeared, anticipating their approaching meals), a man on foot was observed to come from the city with the utmost speed. On reaching the spot of death, he with violence ran from corpse to corpse, as it to seek a well-known face—roughly he seized the heads of each in his hands, and on examination, rudely let them fall: at length he came to one stretched upon the grass, clad in silken robes, stiff with gold, stiffer with blood, and at the first glance, shrieked and grinned the horrid laugh of gratified revenge.

Kneeling on one knee, he took out his knife and stooped; he rose and held up that knife, and on it was stuck the bleeding head thus severed from the body—the head of Elkanah, whose serpent mouth was yet filled with dust. It was Omar, the Arab—Omar, the half-naked Arab, still wearing his emerald chain, his silken girdle, and golden bracelet.

I have it! he cried, running wildly through the camp, and up the hills, and through the plains; I have the head I swore I would—I have the eyes that scowled upon me, the tongue that called me robber.

Not far from the brink of the river (the crimsoned river, alas!) lay the bodies of Hyrcanius, Timagenes, Caleb, and Statirus, and at a few paces distant, the headless corpse of Victorinus, and the mangled form of Orodes, both brought with Zenobia prisoners from the Euphrates.

Orodes yet breathed, for none would in cool blood strike this aged patriot, whose death was every instant expected. His face was towards the Roman camp, until he whispered a soldier, who, aided by Sandarion, turned him on his right side, and he was then in face of Palmyra, on which he gazed in tender, dying languishment : Thank thee, my friends, sighed Orodes, and expired.

. Between the slaughtered remains of Balista and Valerius lay extended on the sands, the gallant Zabdas, his breast and limbs exhibiting wounds innumerable, gotten in his attempt to force his way to the tent of Zenobia; his name though the first on the list, not one could be found to hasten his death. No dishonourable blow shall Zabdas receive, said Claudian, running forward, and covering him with his shield, as he perceived the soldiers advancing with lingering pace towards the wounded, expiring general, in order reluctantly to dispatch him—he shall not die the death of a criminal, but that of a soldier; and whilst Marcellus supported on his knee the head of Zabdas, Claudian ran and fetched water from the river, of which when he had tasted, he took the hand of Claudian—When boys, we fought for the honour of Palmyra, and I was overcome by thee—O Palmyra!

Noble Zabdas! said Claudian, as he grasped the cold hand, and gazed on the dead features, thy honoured ashes shall be inurned by me, and never depart from beneath my roof.

Antiochus, who had long strolled from place to place, watching with calm despair the last convulsions of each expiring friend, on witnessing the death of Zabdas, and seeing that no more of his friends remained alive, went and seated himself as near the door of Zenobia's tent as the guard would permit him, his hands joined, his lips closed, his eyes fixed upon that door. Marcellus and Claudian approached him, but vain their endeavours to obtain his notice, until seeing Sandarion draw near, they observed, that could *he* but be prevailed upon to solicit the emperor's indulgence, Antiochus might be permitted to see his daughter. Antiochus heard the words, and with silent agony clasped the knees of Sandarion.

Art thou Zenobia's father? demanded the tribune. I will intercede for thee with Aurelian, but give thee no hope, for he hath forbidden, under pain of death, all communication with thy daughter.

Sandarion disengaged himself from Antiochus, and entered the tent of Aurelian, but almost instantly returned, filled with alarm and consternation; he was followed by one, who putting a trumpet to his lips, blew three loud and distinct charges, upon which, as instantly, a Roman phalanx was formed, which advanced in admirable order, although a few minutes before, the soldiers composing it had been dispersed through the plains.

Guard the tent of the Syrian queen! commanded Sandarion aloud, as he sprung upon his foaming charger; her life is threatened by the barbarians. At the same moment, from the opposite side of the hills, a band of Moorish and other auxiliary troops poured down, and attempted to carry the tent by storm. Give her to our vengeance! vociferated their gigantic leader; the cause of the siege, the cause of our sufferings: but for her rebellion, we had not met this burning sky, these blistering sands, and scorching rocks—let her die, let her be rent to atoms!—Charge! roared the appalling Sandarion, and those of the mutineers that did not fly, were crushed and trampled beneath the horses' hoofs.

The evening came—the moon arose—haste and climb over the hills, O welcome planet; or rather linger, and come not to behold the change that hath taken place since thou last shedst thy beams upon Palmyra.—Dost thou, O moon, turn pale with horror? dost wrap thy face in clouds? are these drops of rain that fall, tears of pity at witnessing a sight like this?

The Syrians hiding in caves and sepulchres, the Jews cloathed in sackcloth, the Christians kneeling in dust—shepherds, herds, and flocks turned at every corner, when trying to escape, by shouting soldiers; every gate, and door, and house of Palmyra open; the watch lights burning in the sockets; cattle roaming into the streets; horses, mules, and camels, though saddled and laden, browsing on the hills without leader or rider! They seek pasture in fields and plains covered with the slaughtered bodies of the besieger and the besieged, and half-extinguished funeral piles; men wander to and fro in sullen despair; women, weary of tears, strive to comfort their children, and keep them from straying;

looking at the enemy, who, in different groups, carelessly feed or slumber, yet unable themselves to feed or sleep.

No longer is the Temple of the Sun the object of Palmyrenian worship, the tent enclosing their adored Zenobia engrosses universal attention; with jealous eye they watch the approach of any of the barbarian troops, and at the instant inform the Roman—O wondrous contradiction! thus compelled to look to the enemy for the protection of their queen!

O, said they, he will relent—Aurelian will yet be softened to humanity; when he sees how she is by us beloved, how idolized, he will restore her to Palmyra.

The sickening moon disappeared, the dawn blushed, and the sun hastened in its turn, to behold what further changes since he last went down. At the first ray of that sun upon the tops of the mountains, a loud charge of clarions was heard, and the same moment the Roman guard, which had been all night stationed in deep and awful silence around the tent of the queen, broke their ranks—they negligently piled their arms, and whilst some dispersed to prepare their morning repast, others threw themselves on the ground to indulge in sleep.

The Palmyrenians rushed to that tent, now no longer guarded; it was thrown open to them, and they found it empty; that of Aurelian was at the same time struck, and nor emperor nor Zenobia was seen—all around was solitary and deserted—Where, O where, cried the frantic people, running to and fro, O where is she?—Gone, replied Sandarion; at sun-set she was removed hence, and is now with the emperor and his armies on her way to Europe.

Sorrow and despair is useless, ye Palmyrenians, added Marcellus, ye will behold Zenobia no more, she being reserved for the emperor's triumph.—Never! interrupted Antiochus, rouzed at length from the stupor of grief to the excess of wrath and bitter disappointment; never will she live to see that hour—the asp, the steel, the poisonous drug will avert that last dishonour.

Were Zenobia, Antiochus, of our faith, said Claudian, to such doubtless she would have recourse, but as a Jewess, by some said a Christian, she will rather endure temporal affliction; moreover, grieved am I to say, that Aurelian, imitating the policy of Cæsar, flatters thy daughter with a hope (his triumph over) of suffering her to return hither, though with limited power, which perhaps Zenobia credulously believes.

Thou dost not do our emperor justice, Claudian, interrupted Sandarion, for such his admiration of this matchless queen, that I know his promise to have been sincere.

O, on hearing these words of Sandarion, how quick the transition from despair to hope and joy in the breast of Antiochus, and that of every Palmyrenian present.

Then, my friends, added Marcellus,

let me predict, ere I with Claudian leave you to follow our emperor, that Palmyra, like this young palm (and he pointed to a solitary tree near where they stood, the branches of which were half covered by a ponderous shield,) though now depressed by the superior arm of Rome, may yet revive and flourish, the ornament and wonder of the East.

A Scythian trooper, who heard the words, put forth his iron hand, and tearing up the sapling by the roots, long held it up on high, with malicious exultation to the Palmyrenians, then threw it into the flames of a neighbouring fire, upon which Antiochus intently gazed, until leaves, branches, trunk, and root were wholly consumed.

The gallant Romans disdaining to notice this savage and ungenerous action, Marcellus added, You are still a rich and powerful state; your population great, your commerce flourishing; no longer an empire it is true, but a free commonwealth. Be aware, however, that though governed by your own senate, you are to be henceforward considered a Roman province, and to admit for a time a Roman garrison, of which Sandarion here is by Aurelian appointed governor. You may yourselves judge of the emperor's favourable intentions towards you, and the dependance he places on your fidelity, when informed that the garrison is only to consist of five hundred archers and four hundred cavalry.

For the sake then of yourselves, your families, and city, said Claudian, treat the Romans left among you not as enemies, but as friends and defenders; at the end of a limited period they will be wholly withdrawn, and Zenobia restored to her country, though not her throne; monarchs as great as yours have been shown through Rome in triumph, and to be conquered by Rome is no degradation.

Return then to your city and your homes, ye men of Palmyra, added Marcellus; though not as great as ere this our attack, ye may be happier, for on earth no city exceeds, nay equals, yours; we heard of its fame, but expectation is far surpassed; its customs and manners Roman, its architecture Grecian, embellished and softened by Asiatic delicacy, where on the globe is its equal? Enter then once more your gates; be kind to the Christians favoured by the emperor, be faithful to Sandarion and his troops thus left to your mercy, and as you treat them, expect to be treated by Aurelian.

Now then, Palmyra, dear hapless city! turning away our face, we look to Rome. O Rome, rejoice not in thy conquest, exult not over thy illustrious captive, but receive her honorably, tenderly —lament her fall, pity her youth, her loveliness; reflect how gloriously she hath swayed, till of late, the sceptre of the East, and compassionate her destiny.

Generous Rome! it did compassionate, it did not exult—nor shouts, nor acclamations were heard; the covered litters passed in silence through the streets, and stopped unattended by idlers or curious spectators, at a palace near the capitol. Alas! they well knew, that curiosity would be amply gratified at the coming triumph.

From the entrance of the queen, her sons, and women into that palace, to the hour when they were brought forth to appear in that splendid triumph, on all that approached them, who were but few, by the emperor's command, was imposed the silence of the grave. Such their strict obedience to this order, that the captives suspected their Roman attendants had been purposely deprived of the organs of speech; but the triumph once over, silence was at an end, their house was no longer a prison, they were free to leave it, and visitors were free to enter, for Aurelian had nothing more to fear.

Zenobia, her feet and hands loaded

with golden chains, her sons fainting beneath theirs, mounted in that same chariot, built by Firmius to carry her triumphantly through Rome, was led in triumph by her conqueror, who well knew she never had willingly done thus, had she but known the events that had taken place since her departure from Asia.

The procession over, on her return to the palace, her limbs still confined by chains, she repaired to a distant inner room, which, high, gloomy, and unadorned, resembled more the cell of a prison, than the apartment of a mansion in imperial Rome, and there, prostrate on the earth, Zenobia appeared to close the dreadful humiliation she had undergone.

Sabina, Mariam, and Terentia, who still with fond respect clung to her fortunes, in silence attempted to unfasten her chains, on which their tears fell, but too firmly rivetted for such weak hands to unlock, they relieved her drooping head of the oppressive, and now degraded crown, the weighty robes massive with gold and invaluable jewels, her collars, bracelets, sandals, and ornaments of every description, and leaving her reclined upon a couch, went to seek proper assistance.

Victoria, though a Syrian by birth, as the wife of the Roman Claudian, had been spared appearing in the triumph: not willingly, but by the authority of her husband, was she constrained to abandon Zenobia in that hour of affliction, but no authority could now prevent her taking her place by the bed of suffering royalty.

She was kneeling beside Zenobia, who, through fatigue and agony of mind, appeared as if fainting, when Herennianus and Timolaus, their beauteous innocent faces bathed in tears, entered the room; divested of their robes and symbols of slavery, they silently approached the couch, one at the feet of his mother, the other at her head, and softly taking up the ponderous chains, still fastened to her wrists and ancles, they passed them round their own necks, thus easing her of their weight.

Zenobia, opening her eyes, beheld them encumbered thus, and in speechless emotion raised those agonized eyes to heaven; from her children, she looked gratefully at Victoria, and then around, as seeking her youngest child. A soldier at the instant entered, bearing on his arm a burden wrapped in a brown mantle.

I am sent to know, said he, whether you will have the body burned or interred? The queen, Victoria, and the princes looked at the man, in wonder at his meaning; again he repeated his message, and a third time asked, what should be done with the corpse, when, irritated by their silence, he threw down his burden, and retired—the youths ran towards it, and with a wild shriek caught it in their arms.

Vaballathus! our brother! but newly killed—still warm, O perhaps still living!

—Softly, my children, said Victoria, bring it hither—if life remains, alarm the palace, and send for help; if dead, take it hence, ere thy mother again revive.

Victoria examined the body, and found the heart deeply stabbed; Refrain, dear boys, she said, from useless lamentation, and take this murdered innocent to Sabina and the women within; impose silence on them, and return hither: if you are also marked as victims, be your bed of death the side of your mother.

Herennianus clasped the body in his arms, and, assisted by Timolaus, who in vain strove to stifle his gushing tears, quitted the apartment, but when they entered that wherein were assembled the captive Palmyrenians, they could no longer refrain their grief: with sobs and lamentations they mourned over Vaballathus, and hung in anguish on each other's neck.

On their offering to return where they had left their mother, they were prevented by Claudian, who hastily entered, terror and alarm in his countenance; taking a hand of each of the princes, he led them away as hastily, and in profound silence.

Where, O where is this hapless queen? demanded a voice from without the door of Zenobia's room, and Marcellus appeared; Victoria pointed to the senseless form of Zenobia, and still, but in vain, continued to administer restoratives.

What, O what hath happened to produce this unforeseen and cruel change in Aurelian? enquired Victoria of her husband Claudian, who now joined them; Vaballathus is murdered, and doubtless his brothers are to share his fate; is this the promise of your emperor? this his fidelity to the oath he took, of restoring Zenobia and her children to Palmyra?

O Victoria, replied Claudian, had Palmyra still existed, Aurelian would have kept his oath, but on this earth there is no longer a Palmyra. Reflect on the day we reached the shores of Asia, ready to embark for Europe: on that day, a soldier arrived in our camp, whose dire intelligence was conveyed in but few words: 'Emperor,' said he, 'Palmyra has revolted; Antiochus, the father of Zenobia, is proclaimed king, and Sandarion and thy garrison are massacred; of the nine hundred Romans left in that place I only have escaped the sword.'

True; alas! added Marcellus, we were present. The soldier had scarcely ceased speaking, when Aurelian, at the head of thirty thousand troops, galloped from the camp breathing vengeance and extermination against the hapless, the faithless city. An eagle on a nest of rejoicing sparrows he fell; Palmyra was taken and sacked; the whole of the inhabitants of both sexes, of every rank and age, were put to death, and the buildings set on fire; houses, palaces, churches, synagogues, and temples, all were in flames; molten gold and silver mingled with the blood of the slaughtered people flowed through the streets; even Aurelian himself could not restrain the fury of his soldiers, and though he commanded, nay, implored them to spare the Temple of the Sun, it was destroyed by the engines of war; nothing now remains but its stupendous and magnificent ruins.

And was Antiochus also slain? demanded Victoria.— The first, replied Claudian, none were spared but the Christians; these, having remonstrated in vain with the Palmyrenians, on their treacherous and cruel design against the humane, though rough Sandarion, and the well-inclined garrison, timely removed themselves from Palmyra to Emessa. From thence, under the guidance of Theodosius their patriarch (who was found at the storming of the place perishing in the dungeons of the city), they will hereafter be permitted by Aurelian to settle at Jerusalem.

The severity of the 'emperor towards this fallen queen, continued, Marcellus, proceeds from suspicion that she was the secret agent that caused the massacre of his brave troops, and favourite Sandarion. Thus Palmyra is razed; and who the author of her destruction?—Not the Roman, but the remains of that pernicious faction, which first advised Zenobia to act contrary to the wisdom and justice of Odenathus.

She revives, said Victoria, be not seen, let me alone tell to her ear this mournful intelligence; she is already acquainted with the death of all her friends, Orodes, Zabdas, Longinus—she hath already seen the body of her slaughtered child Vaballathus, *that* came upon her unprepared and hath thus affected her; but this death of her kingdom, this total annihilation of all her hopes, I take upon myself to make known.—Alas! however gentle my caution, I anticipate the consequence, for is not the fate of Palmyra and of Zenobia one?

Claudian and Marcellus retired; Zenobia recovered, and slowly looked around for her living sons, then at Victoria in speechless enquiry of what had become of them, Victoria understanding the look went to seek the princes, and Zenobia long remained alone.

Again the door opened; a door which seemed to her that of fate, and a stranger clad in long loose robes appeared at the entrance, his feet naked, his head uncovered, his sunken cheek most pale, his eye most languid, and his pale lips trembling with emotion: the staff fell from his grasp, he uttered a sigh of agony as he looked upon Zenobia thus, and rushing forward, seized her cold, her faded, and enchained hand; she felt it moistened with the drops of tenderness.

Theodosius! she cried, and for the first time since she had wept upon the marble statue of Odenathus, burst into tears: her tears fell upon the sacred head of him, who, when she was enthroned, had abhorred to bow the worshipping knee before her, who had refused undue homage to sceptred authority, of him who had declared he never would forsake her.

Theodosius! O my father! and am I

still remembered of thee?—Remembered! he replied, pitied, most honoured: said I not that, when deprived of empire, parents, children, friends, liberty, almost of life, that I would never forsake thee? Did I not promise to stand by thy bed of misery and of death, O thou beloved lost one! and whisper to thy breaking heart comfort and salvation?

With clasped hands and adoring look to the God of mercy, who thus seemed to make another tender of forgiveness, she glided from the couch, and aided by Victoria, who shortly returned, knelt in humble supplication; at the same time authorizing the patriarch by a sign to assist her with his prayers.

Ere I comply, Zenobia, said he, say, should Aurelian offer to restore thee to thy throne and people, with undiminished power on the express condition, that thou solemnly abjurest Christianity, what would be thy choice?—Death rather than compliance, was the answer; and supporting her weak and exhausted frame upon the bosom of Victoria, she long continued in silent prayer, fervent as sincere.

Once more placed upon the couch, she addressed Theodosius, her voice faltering and low, Thou alone canst understand my present feelings; through my wounded soul glides the healing balm of consolation, and the glad hope of forgiveness: more an inhabitant of heaven than earth I at this moment feel, better prepared for the life to come, than a return to sovereign power.

Zenobia, said Theodosius solemnly, yet with affection, thou hast had the merit of renouncing empire for the sake of heaven, and be thy future life devoted to the exercise of private duties, preparing the way to that heaven. Now art thou able, hast thou fortitude, say, hast thou sufficient strength of mind to hear from me the awful truth, ere it can burst like thunder on thee, from the lips of a cruel and vindictive enemy? But, my child, thou wilt spare me the recital, thou wilt divine what my tongue cannot utter.—I know, said Zenobia, that I have lost my youngest boy: I saw his lifeless mangled bosom, but my two elder are living; at least they were, ere at that sight my eyes closed; they supported my fetters; they were at my side: Timolaus, Herennianus, my sons, where are they?

Be calm, said Theodosius, I did not allude to them —My friends, I already know, are all massacred. Is my father then—but what evil can have befallen him? If removed by death (for he was aged) then indeed must I lament in sorrow, that having lived to behold my loss of power, he should not have been spared to witness its recovery: I fondly hoped my father would have been the first to welcome me, my children, and my captive subjects back to Palmyra.

To Palmyra! said the patriarch hiding his face in his hand.—Even so, returned Zenobia amazed, canst thou be ignorant of the promise made me by the emperor? of the terms on which alone I consented to appear a chained prisoner in his triumph? had he made my return to my own, now more than ever beloved Palmyra the conditions, I would gladly, as Valerian to Sapor, have daily bowed my neck his footstool.

O Zenobia! exclaimed Victoria, embracing her and bursting into tears.—Dear and honoured queen! said Theodosius again kneeling and taking her hand. All pale aghast and convulsed, she looked alternately at each.

Speak, she said, half rising, and in a voice so low, so faint, that it could hardly be distinguished, speak, nor thus longer torture me, for no torture equals that of suspense; tell me at once, that my elder children are also slain by Aurelian, and I rush, a distracted mother, through the streets of Rome, invoking the vengeance of the Romans, on the barbarous tyrant whom I prophecy will not long outlive my murdered boy; murder awaits him! Say that my father is dead, and I devote myself to regret, and cloathe me in mourning; but say not, O say not that my Palmyra is no more, that my people are slaughtered, that my city is in ashes, or my heart breaks.

Palmyra is no more! exclaimed a tremendous voice: thy people are slaughtered; thy city is in ashes.

They turned, and saw, leaning negligently against the door-post, a gigantic figure, habited in cloth of gold;—with legs crossed, arms folded in purple robe of exquisite die, and head encircled by a brilliant diadem surmounted with the laurel crown of victory —it was Aurelian.

The swollen heart of Zenobia sank within her; the springs of life were broken at their sources; the spirit fled! Victoria received her last sigh; Theodosius her last look.

THE END.

J. Dennett, Printer, Leather Lane, Holborn, London.

This book is given special protection for the reason
indicated below:

Autograph
Association
Condition
Cost
Edition
Fine binding
Format
Giftbook
Illustration
Miniature book
✓Original binding or covers
Presentation
Scarcity
Subject

L82—1M—11.51—4862

CPSIA information can be obtained at www.ICGtesting.com
Printed in the USA
LVOW10s2115240116

472069LV00022B/2212/P